A Tori Amos Collection

Tales of a Librarian

Cover photograph by Thierry le Goues

Published 2003 by Amsco Publications,
A Division of Music Sales Corporation, New York

Order No. AM 979176
US International Standard Book Number: 0.8256.2875.X
UK International Standard Book Number: 1.84449.339.3

Exclusive Distributors:
Music Sales Corporation
257 Park Avenue South, New York, NY 10010 USA
Music Sales Limited
8/9 Frith Street, London W1D 3JB England
Music Sales Pty. Limited
120 Rothschild Street, Rosebery, Sydney, NSW 2018, Australia

Printed in the United States of America by
Vicks Lithograph and Printing Corporation

Amsco Publications
New York/London/Paris/Sydney/Copenhagen/Berlin/Tokyo/Madrid

Precious Things

so I ran faster
but it caught me here
yes my loyalties turned
like my ankle
in the seventh grade
running after BILLY
running after the rain

these precious things
Let them bleed
Let them wash away
these precious things let them break
their hold on me

he said you're really an ugly girl
but I like the way you play
and I died
but I thanked him
can you believe that
sick. holding on to his picture
dressing up every day
I wanna smash the faces of those beautiful BOYS
those christian boys
so you can made me cum
that doesn't make you Jesus

I remember yes
in my peach party dress
no one dared
no one cared
to tell me where the pretty girls are
those demigods
with their NINE-INCH nails
and little fascist panties
tucked inside the heart
of every nice girl

Angels

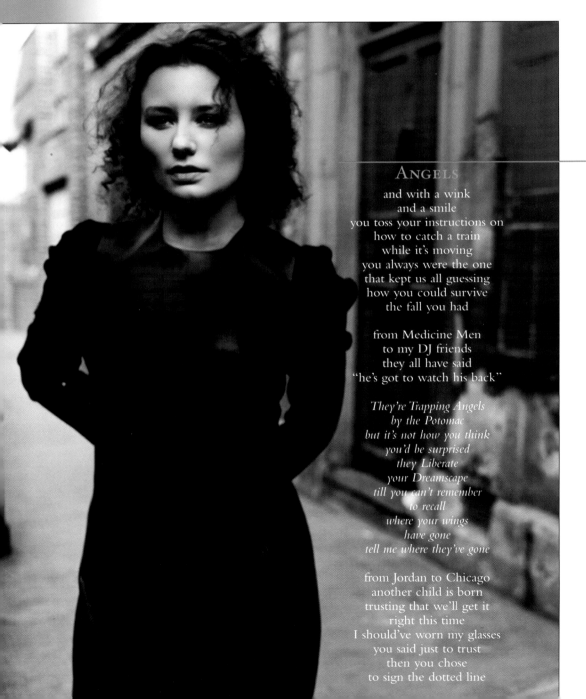

and with a wink
and a smile
you toss your instructions on
how to catch a train
while it's moving
you always were the one
that kept us all guessing
how you could survive
the fall you had

from Medicine Men
to my DJ friends
they all have said
"he's got to watch his back"

They're Trapping Angels
by the Potomac
but it's not how you think
you'd be surprised
they Liberate
your Dreamscape
till you can't remember
to recall
where your wings
have gone
tell me where they've gone

from Jordan to Chicago
another child is born
trusting that we'll get it
right this time
I should've worn my glasses
you said just to trust
then you chose
to sign the dotted line

from Modern Magdalenes
to my DJ friends
they all have said
"he's got to watch his back"

They're Trapping Angels
by the Potomac
but it's not how you think
you'd be surprised
they Liberate
your Dreamscape
till you can't remember
to recall
where your wings
have gone

Before I close my eyes at night
I can still see you smilin'
Before the Truth was
Buried Alive
did we prize it
Before you change the world
maybe boy you should change
your girl

They're Trapping Angels
by the Potomac
They're Trapping Angels
Lord I know this
They're Trapping Angels
by the Potomac
But we're getting closer
I said we're getting closer
to where they've gone
tell me where they've gone
now it won't be long

Silent All These Years

excuse me but can I be you for a while
my DOG won't bite if you sit real still
I got the anti-Christ in the kitchen yellin' at me again
yeah I can hear that

been saved again by the garbage truck
I got something to say you know but NOTHING comes
yes I know what you think of me you never shut up
yeah I can hear that

but what if I'm a mermaid
in these jeans of his with her name still on it
hey but I don't care
cause sometimes I said sometimes I hear my voice and it's been
HERE silent all these years

so you found a girl who thinks really deep thoughts
what's so amazing about really deep thoughts
Boy you best pray that I bleed real soon
how's that thought for you

my scream got lost in a paper cup
you think there's a heaven where some screams have gone
I got 25 bucks and a cracker do you think it's enough
to get us there

years go by will I still be waiting
for somebody else to understand
years go by if I'm stripped of my beauty
and the orange clouds raining in my head
years go by will I choke on my tears
till finally there is nothing left
One more casualty
you know we're to EASY easy easy

well I love the way we communicate
your eyes focus on my funny lip shape
Let's hear what you think of me now but baby don't look up
the sky is falling

your MOTHER shows up in a nasty dress
It's your turn now to stand where I stand
Everybody lookin' at you here take hold of my hand
yeah I can hear them

Cornflake Girl

Never was a Cornflake Girl
thought that was a good solution
hangin' with the raisin girls
she's gone to the other side
givin' us a yo heave ho
things are getting kind of gross
and I go at sleepy time

This is not really happening
You bet your life it is
You bet your life it is
Peel out the Watchword
just Peel out the Watchword

she knows what's goin' on
seems we got a cheaper feel now
all the sweeteaze are gone
Gone to the other side
with my encyclopedia
they musta paid her a nice price
she's puttin' on her string bean love

Rabbit where'd you put the keys girl
to close this door I know it's so easy
Rabbit where'd you put the keys
to close this door I know it's so easy
and the man with the golden gun thinks he knows so much
thinks he knows so much
thinks he knows so much
Rabbit where'd you put the keys girl

Mary

Everybody wants something from you
Everybody want a piece of Mary
Lush valley all dressed in green
just ripe for the picking
god I want to get you out of here
you can ride in a pink Mustang
when I think of what we've done to you
Mary, can you hear me?
Growing up isn't always fun
they tore your dress
and stole your ribbons
They see you cry
They lick their lips
well Butterflies don't belong in nets
Mary
can you hear me?
Mary
you're bleeding
Mary
don't be afraid
we're just waking up
and I hear help is on the way
Mary
can you hear me?
Mary
like Jimi said
Mary
don't be afraid

"cause even the wind
even the wind cries your name"
Everybody wants you sweetheart
Everybody got a dream of glory
Las Vegas got a pinup girl
they got her armed
as they buy and sell her
Rivers of milk running dry
can't you hear the dolphins crying
what'll we do when our babies scream
Fill their mouths with some acid rain
Mary
can you hear me?
Mary
you're bleeding
Mary
don't be afraid
we're just waking up
and I hear help is on the way
Mary
can you hear me?
Mary
like Jimi said
Mary
don't be afraid
"cause even the wind
even the wind cries your name"

God

God sometimes you just don't come through
God sometimes you just don't come through
Do you need a woman to look after you
God sometimes you just don't come through

you make pretty daisies
pretty daisies love
I gotta find what you're doing about things here
a few witches burning gets a little toasty here
I gotta find why you always go when the wind blows

God sometimes you just don't come through
God sometimes you just don't come through
Do you need a woman to look after you
God sometimes you just don't come through

tell me you're crazy maybe then I'll understand
you got your 9 iron in the back seat just in case
heard you've gone south well Babe you love your new 4 wheel
I gotta find why you always go when the wind blows

'give not thy strength unto women
nor thy ways to that which destroyeth kings' Proverbs 31:3

will you even tell her if you decide to make the sky fall
will you even tell her if you decide to make the sky

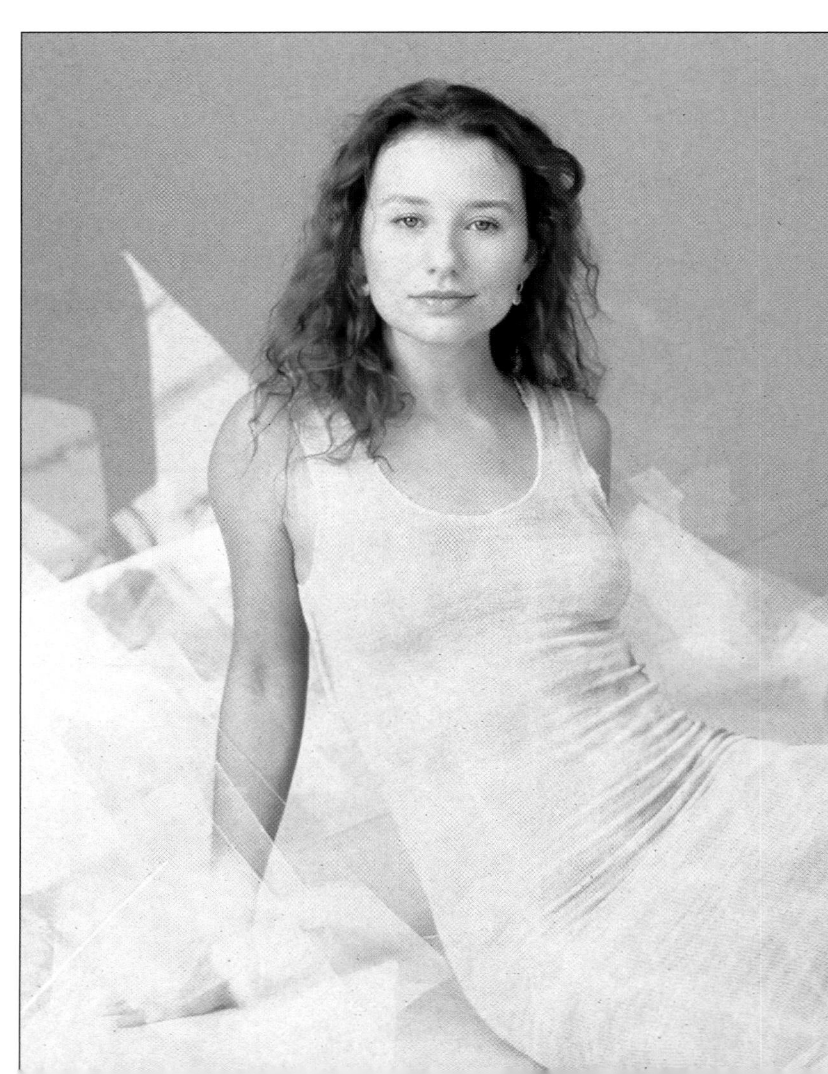

Winter

snow can wait
I forgot my mittens
wipe my nose, get my new boots on
I get a little warm in my heart
when I think of winter
I put my hand in my father's glove
I run off where the DRIFTS GET DEEPER
sleeping beauty trips me with a frown
I hear a voice,
"you must learn to stand up for yourself
cause I can't always be around"
he says...

when you gonna make up your mind
when you gonna love you as much as I do
when you gonna make up your mind
'cause things are gonna CHANGE so fast
all the white horses are still in bed
I tell you that I'll always want you near
you say that things change, my dear

boys get discovered
as winter MELTS
flowers competing for the sun
years go by
and I'm here still waiting
withering where some snowman was
mirror, mirror
where's the crystal palace
but I only can see myself
SKATING around the truth who I am
but I know, Dad, the ice is getting thin

hair is grey
and the fires are burning
so many dreams on the shelf
you say "I wanted you to be PROUD of me"
I always wanted that myself

when you gonna make up your mind
when you gonna love you as much as I do
when you gonna make up your mind
'cause things are gonna CHANGE so fast
all the white horses have gone ahead
I tell you that I'll always want you near
you say that things change, my dear
all the white horses

Spark

She's addicted to nicotine patches
She's addicted to nicotine patches
She's afraid of the light in the dark
6:58 are you sure where my spark is
Here
Here
Here
She's convinced she could hold back a glacier
(between cotton balls and xylophones)
but she couldn't keep Baby alive
(I'm getting old)
doubting if there's a woman in there somewhere
Here
Here
Here
You say you don't want it again and again
but you don't you don't really mean it
You say you don't want it
this circus we're in
but you don't you don't really mean it
you don't you don't really mean it

If the Divine master plan is perfection
(swing low)
maybe next I'll give Judas a try
(swing low sweet chariot)
Trusting my soul to the ice cream assassin
Here
Here
Here

How may fates turn around in the overtime
Ballerinas that have fins that you'll never find
you thought that you were the bomb
yeah well so did I
Say you don't want it
Say you don't want it
Say you don't want it again and again

She's addicted to nicotine patches
She's afraid of the light in the dark
6:58 are you sure where my spark is
Here

Way Down

Maybe I'm the afterglow
'cause I'm with the band you know
don't you hear the laughter on the way down

Yes I am the anchorman
dining here with Son of Sam
a hair too much to chat of on the way down

Gonna meet a great big star
gonna drive his great big car
gonna have it all here on the way down

the way down
the way down
she knows
let's go
way down
way down
the way down
she knows

Professional Widow

slag pit
stag shit
honey bring it close to my lips
yes
don't blow those brains yet
we gotta be big boy
we gotta be big

starfucker just like my Daddy
just like my Daddy selling his baby
just like my Daddy
gonna strike a deal make him feel
like a Congressman
it runs in the family
gonna strike a deal make him feel
like a Congressman
it runs in the family

rest your shoulders Peaches and Cream
everywhere a Judas as far as you can see
beautiful angel
calling "we got every re-run of Muhammad Ali"
prism perfect
honey bring it close to your lips
yes
what is termed a landslide of principle
proportion boy it gotta be big boy

Mother Mary
china white
brown may be sweeter
she will supply
she will supply
she will supply
she will supply
give me peace love
and a hard cock

Mr. Zebra

hello Mr Zebra
can I have your sweater
cause it's cold cold cold
in my hole hole hole
Ratatouille Strychnine
sometimes she's a friend of mine
with a gigantic whirlpool
that will blow your mind

hello Mr Zebra
ran into some confusion with a Mrs. Crocodile
furry mussels marching on
she thinks she's Kaiser Wilheim
or a civilized syllabub
to blow your mind
figure it out
she's a goodtime fella
she got a little fund to fight for Moneypenny's rights
figure it out
she's a goodtime fella
'too bad the burial was premature' she said
and smiled

Crucify

Every finger in the room is pointing at me
I wanna spit in their faces
then I get afraid what that could bring
I got a bowling ball in my stomach
I got a desert in my mouth
figures that my COURAGE would choose to sell out now.

I've been looking for a savior in these dirty streets
Looking for a savior beneath these dirty sheets
I've been raising up my hands
Drive another nail in
just what GOD needs
one more victim

why do we crucify ourselves
every day I crucify myself
nothing I do is good enough for you
Crucify myself
every day I crucify myself
and my HEART is sick of being in chains

Got a kick for a dog beggin' for LOVE
I gotta have my suffering
so that I can have my cross
I know a cat named Easter
he says will you ever learn
you're just an empty cage girl if you kill the bird

I've been looking for a savior in these dirty streets
Looking for a savior beneath these dirty sheets
I've been raising up my hands
Drive another nail in
got enough GUILT to start
my own religion

please be
save me
I CRY

Me And A Gun

5am Friday morning Thursday night far from sleep
I'm still up and driving can't go home obviously
So I'll just change direction cause they'll soon know where I live
and I wanna live
got a full tank and some chips
It was me and a gun and a man on my back
and I sang "holy holy" as he buttoned down his pants
You can laugh it's kinda funny the things you think in times like these
but I haven't seen BARBADOS so I must get out of this
Yes I wore a slinky red thing
Does that mean I should spread for you, your friends
Your father, Mr Ed
me and a gun and a man on my back
but I haven't seen BARBADOS so I must get out of this
and I know what this means
me and Jesus a few years back used to hang
and he said "it's your choice babe just remember
I don't think you'll be back in 3 days time so you choose well"
Tell me what's right
Is it my right to be on my stomach of Fred's Seville
me and a gun and a man on my back
but I haven't seen BARBADOS so I must get out of this
and do you know CAROLINA
where the biscuits are soft and sweet
These things go through your head when there's a man on your back
and you're pushed flat on your stomach
it's not a classic Cadillac

Bliss

Father, I killed my monkey
I let it out to
taste the sweet of spring
wonder if I will wander out
test my tether to
see if I'm still free
from you

steady as it comes
right down
to you
I've said it all
so maybe we're a Bliss
of another kind

lately, I'm in to circuitry
what it means to be
made of you but not enough for you
and I wonder if
you can bilocate is that
what I taste
your supernova juice
you know it's true I'm part of you

steady as it comes
right down to you
I've said it all

so maybe you're a 4 horse engine
with a power drive
a hot kachina who wants into mine
take it with your terracide

we're a Bliss
of another kind

Playboy Mommy

In my platforms
I hit the floor
fell face down
didn't help my brain out
Then the baby came
before I found
the magic how
to keep her happy
I never was the fantasy
of what you want
wanted me to be

Don't judge me so harsh little girl,
so you got a playboy mommy
But when you tell 'em my name and
you want to cross that Bridge
all on your own
Little girl they'll do you no harm
cause they know
your playboy mommy
But when you tell 'em my name
from here to Birmingham I got a few friends

I never was there
was there when it counts
I get my way
you're so like me
You seemed ashamed
Ashamed that I was
a good friend of American Soldiers
I'll say it loud here by your grave
those angels can't
ever take my place

Don't judge me so harsh little girl,
you got a playboy mommy
But when you tell 'em my name and
and you want to cross that Bridge
all on your own
Little girl they'll do you no harm
cause they know
your playboy mommy
But you just tell 'em my name
you tell 'em my name
I got a few friends

Somewhere where the orchids grow
I can't find those church bells
that played when you died
played Gloria
talkin' bout
Hosanah

Don't judge me so harsh little girl,
you got a playboy mommy
come home
but when you tell them soldiers
my name
cross that Bridge
all on your own
Little girl they'll
do you no harm
cause they know your playboy mommy
but I'll be home
I'll be home
to take you in my arms

Baker Baker

Baker Baker
baking a cake
make me a day
make me whole again
and I wonder
what's in a day
what's in you cake this time

I guess you heard
he's gone to LA
he says that behind my eyes I'm hiding
and he tells me I pushed him away
that my hearts been hard to find

here there must be something here
there must be something here. here

Baker Baker can you explain
if truly his heart
was made of icing
and I wonder
how mine could taste
maybe we could change his mind

I know you're late
for your next parade
you came to make sure
that I'm not running
well I ran from him
in all kinds of ways
guess it was his turn this time

Time thought I'd made friends with time
Thought we'd be flying
maybe not this time

Baker Baker
baking a cake
make me a day
make me whole again
and I wonder
if he's ok
if you see him say hi

Tear In Your Hand

all the world just stopped now
so you say you don't wanna stay together anymore
let me take a deep breath babe if you need me
me and Neil'll be hangin' out with the DREAM KING

Neil says hi by the way
I don't believe you're leaving cause me and Charles Manson like the same ice cream
I think it's that girl and I think there're pieces of me you've never seen
maybe she's just pieces of me you've never seen well

All the world is
All I am
the black of the blackest ocean
and that tear in your hand
all the world is DANGLIN'... danglin'... danglin' for me DARLIN'
you don't know the power that you have
with that tear in your hand
tear in your hand

maybe I ain't used to maybes smashing in a cold room cutting my hands up every time I touch you
Maybe maybe it's time to wave goodbye now
time to wave goodbye now

caught a ride with the moon
I know I know you well well better than I used to
HAZE all clouded up my mind
in the DAZE of the why it could've never been
so you say and I say you know you're full of wish
and your "baby baby baby babies"
I tell you there're pieces of me you've never seen
maybe she's just pieces of me you've never seen

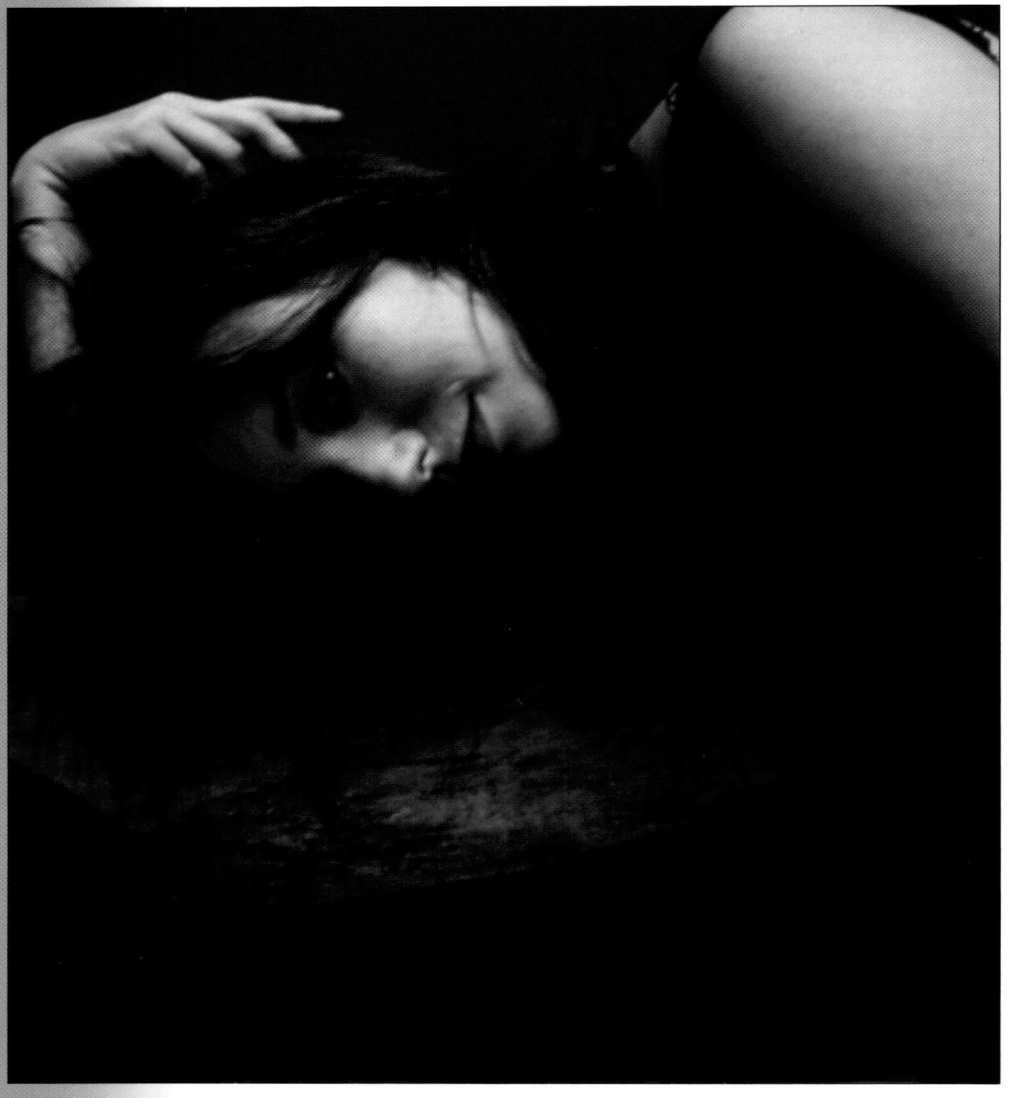

Sweet Dreams

"Lie, lie, lies everywhere" said the Father to the son
You're peppermint breath gonna choke him to death
Daddy watch your little black sheep run
He got knives in his back
Everytime he opens up
You say "He gotta be strong if you want to be a man"
Mister I don't know how you can have
sweet dreams sweet dreams

Land, Land of Liberty we're run by a constipated man
when you live in the past
you refuse to see
when your daughter comes home nine months pregnant
with Five Billion Points of Light
Gonna shine 'em on the face of your friends
They got the earth in a sling
They got the world on her knees
They even got your zipper
Between their teeth
sweet dreams sweet dreams
you say, you say, you say you have 'em
I say that you're a liar
sweet dreams sweet dreams
go on, go on, go on, go on and dream
your house is on fire
Come along now

well well well summer wind
Been catching up with me
"Elephant mind, missy you don't have
you forgettin' to fly, darlin', when you sleep"
I got hazy lazy Susan
takin' turns all over my dreams
I got lizards and snakes
runnin' through my body
Funny how they all have my face
sweet dreams sweet dreams

Jackie's Strength

a Bouvier till her wedding day
shots rang out the police came
mama layed me on the front lawn
and prayed for Jackie's strength
feeling old by 21
never thought my day would come
my bridemaids getting laid I pray for Jackie's strength

make me laugh
say you know what you want
you said we were the real thing
so I show you some more and I learn
what black magic can do
make me laugh
say you know you can turn
me into the real thing
so I show you some more
and I learn

stickers licked on lunch boxes worshipping David Cassidy
yeah I mooned him once on Donna's box
she's still in recovery
sleep-overs Beene's got some pot
you're only popular with anorexia so I turn myself inside out
in hope someone will see

I got lost on my wedding day typical the police came
but virgins always get backstage no matter what they've got to say
if you love enough you'll lie a lot
guess they did in camelot
mama's waiting on my front lawn
I pray I pray I pray
for Jackie's strength

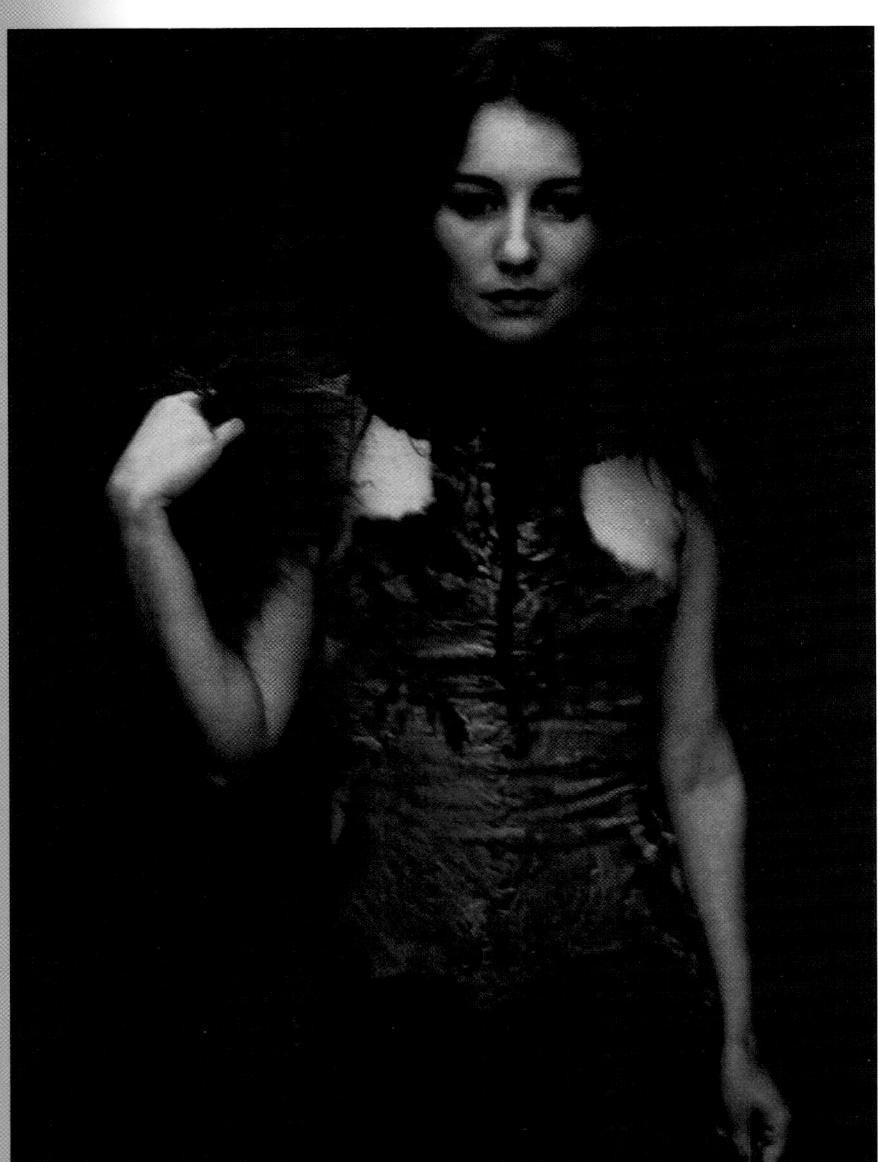

Snow Cherries From France

I knew a boy who would
not share his bike
oh but he let me go sailing
I swore that I
could survive any storm
oh then he let me go

"Can you Launch Rockets from here?"
Boy I've done it for years
right over my head
and when I promised my hand
he promised me back
Snow Cherries from France
all that summer
we traveled the world
never leaving his own back garden
girls I didn't know
just what it could be
oh but he let me go sailing

you question me,
"Can you ride anything?"
Lord do you mean like your mood swings
Invaders and Traders with
the best intentions
may convince you to go
"They look like Pirates from here"
Boy I've been one for years
just keeping my head
and when I promised my hand
you promised me back
Snow Cherries from France

and then one day he said
"Girl it's been nice,
oh but I have to go sailing"
with cinnamon lips
that did not match his eyes
oh then he let me go

Pretty Good Year

Tears on the sleeve of a man
don't wanna be a boy today
heard the eternal footman
bought himself a bike to race

and Greg he writes letters and burns his CDs
they say you were something in those formative years
hold onto nothing as fast as you can
well still pretty good year

Maybe a bright sandy beach
is gonna bring you back
maybe not so now you're off
you're gonna see America
well let me tell you something about America
pretty good year (pretty she is pretty she can be)
some things are melting now
some things are melting now
well what's it gonna take till my baby's alright
what's it gonna take till my baby's alright

and Greg he writes letters with his birthday pen
sometimes he's aware that they're drawing him in
Lucy was pretty your best friend agreed
well still pretty good year

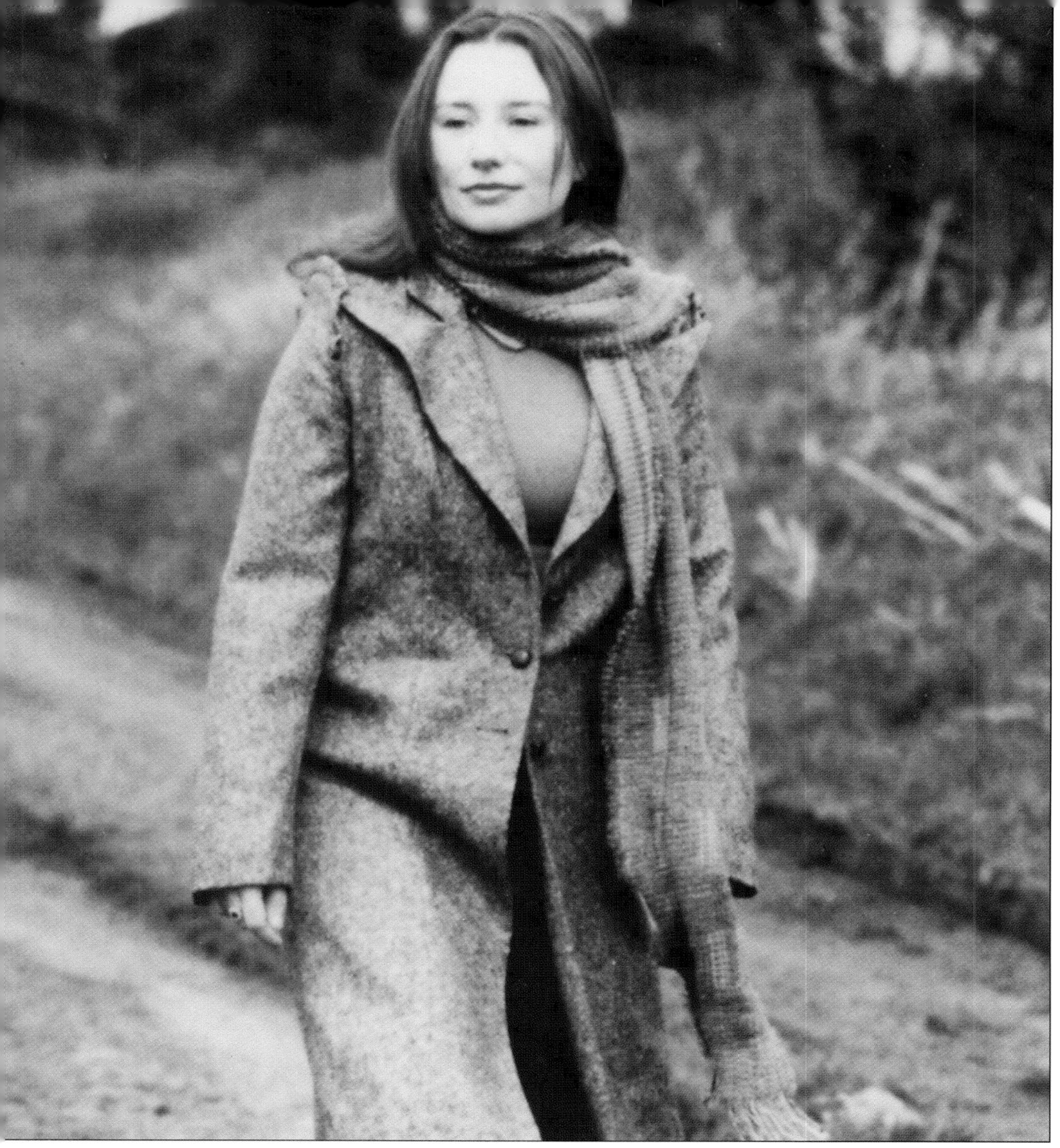

Northern Lad

Had a northern lad
well not exactly had
he moved like the sunset
god who painted that
first he loved my accent
how his knees could bend
I thought we'd be ok
me and my molasses
But I feel something is wrong
But I feel this cake just isn't done
Don't say that you Don't

and if you could see me now
said if you could see me now
girls you've got to know
when it's time to turn the page
when you're only wet
because of the rain
when you're only wet
because of the rain

he don't show much these days
it gets so fucking cold
I loved his secret places
but I can't go anymore
"you change like sugar cane"
says my northern lad
I guess you go too far
when pianos try to be guitars
I feel the west in you
and I feel it falling apart too
Don't say that you Don't

Honey

a little dust never stopped me none he liked my shoes I kept them on
sometimes I can hold my tongue sometimes not
when you just skip-to-loo my darlin'
and you know what you're doin' so don't even

you're just too used to my honey now
you're just too used to my honey

and I think I could leave your world if she was the better girl
so when we died I tried to bribe the undertaker
cause I'm not sure what you're doin' or the reasons
you're just too used to my honey now
you're just too used to my honey

don't bother coming down
I made a friend of the western sky
don't bother coming down
you always liked your Babies tight

turn back one last time love to watch those cowboys ride
but cowboys know cowgirls ride on the Indian side
and you know what you're doin' so don't even

you're just too used to my honey now
you're just too used to my honey

Putting The Damage On

glue
stuck to my shoes
does anyone know why you play with an orange rind
you say you packed my things
and divided what was mine you're off to the mountain top
I say her skinny legs could use sun
but now I'm wishing
for my best impression
of my best Angie Dickinson
but now I've got to worry
cause boy you still look pretty
when you're putting the damage on
yes
when you're putting the damage on

don't make me scratch on you door
I never left you
for a Banjo
I only just turned around for a poodle
and a corvette
and my impression
of my best Angie Dickinson
but now I've got to worry
cause boy you still look pretty
when you're putting the damage on
pretty
when you're putting the damage on

I'm trying not to move
it's just your ghost
passing through
I said
I'm trying not to move
it's just your ghost passing through
it's just your ghost
passing through
and now
I'm quite sure
there's a light in your platoon
I never seen a light move
like yours
can do to me
so now I'm wishing
for my best impression
of my best Angie Dickinson
but now I've got to worry
cause boy you still look pretty
to me
but I've got a place to go
I've got a ticket to your late show
and now I've got to worry cause even still
you sure are pretty
when you're putting the damage on
yes
when you're putting the damage on
you're just so pretty
when you're putting the damage on

Precious Things

Words and Music by Tori Amos

Gmaj7
Asus4 A Asus4 A
grade running after Billy running-after the rain
Em7/D D A/E D/F♯ Bm D G
These precious things Let them bleed let them
melody
mf
Asus4 A Asus4/E A/E A Em7/D D A/E D/F♯ Bm D
wash away These precious things Let them
G Asus4 A Asus4 A
to Coda
Bm6/9
break their hold on me
8
mp

Gmaj7
Asus4
A
Asus4
A
He said you're real - ly an ug -
8
loco
Bm6/9
Gmaj7
ly girl But I like the way you play and I
Asus4
A
Asus4
A
Bm6/9
died But I thanked him Can you be - lieve that sick sick hold - ing on - to his
Gmaj7
A
pic - ture dres - sing up ev - ery day I wan - na smash the

Bm6/9
Gmaj7/B
faces of those beau-ti-ful boys those Chris-tian boys so you can
Asus4
A
Asus4
A
Esus4
E
Esus4
E
D.S. al Coda
make me cum That does-n't make you Je-e-sus
Coda
Bm6/9
G
I I re-mem-ber
Bm11
B9sus4
Bm11
B9sus4
F♯m
Bm/F♯
F♯m7
Bm/F♯
yes In my peach par-ty dress No one
melody

F♯m7
Bm/F♯
F♯m7/C♯
Bm/C♯
Bm6/9
dared no one cared to tell me where the
Gmaj7
A
pret - ty girls are Those dem - i - gods with their
melody
E5
nine inch nails and lit - tle fas - cist pan - ties tucked in - side the heart of ev - ery nice
subito f
Bbass
Dbass
Abass
Ebass
F♯bass
5fr.
7fr.
9fr.
girl
coll' 8

Bbass
Dbass
Abass
Ebass
F♯bass
G bass
F♯bass
coll' 8
Em7/D
D
A/E
D/F♯
Bm
D
G
These pre - cious things Let them bleed let them
melody
mf
Asus4
A
Asus4/E
A/E
Em7/D
D
A/E
D/F♯
Bm
D
wash a - way These pre - cious things Let them
G
Asus4
A
Asus4
A
repeat and fade
break their hold on me

Angels

Words and Music by Tori Amos

Slowly, rhythmic
Am9
D
mp
Am9
D
Am9
D
And with a wink and a smile you toss your in - struc - tions on
From Jor - dan to Chi - ca - go an - oth - er child is born
F
Cadd9
G
how to catch a train while it's mov - ing
trust - ing that we'll get it right this time

Am9
D
You al - ways were the one that kept us all guess - ing
I should have worn my glass - es you said just to trust
F
Cadd9
G
how you could sur - vive the fall you had
then you chose to sign the dot - ted line
Em
Cmaj7
Am7
From Med - i - cine Men
Mod - ern Mag - da lenes
to my D J friends they
Dm
Am
Esus4
E
all have said "he's got to watch his back"
They're trap - ping An -

Bm add9
E/G♯
gels by the Po - to - mac But it's
mf
G
D
F♯sus4
F♯
Bm add9
not how you think you'd be sur - prised They li - ber - ate your dream-
E/G♯
G
D
scape till you can't re - mem - ber to re -
F♯sus4
F♯
Esus2
1.
Cadd9
G/B
call where your wings have gone

A Asus4 Cadd9 G/B A Asus4 A
Tell me where they've gone
2.
Cadd9 G/B A Asus4 A Am9
gone
Be - fore I close my eyes at night
D Am9
I can still see you smil - in' be - fore the truth was bur - ied
D Am9
a - live did we prize it be - fore you change the world

D
may - be boy you should change your girl They're trap - ping An -
Bm add9
E/G♯
gels by the Po - to - mac They're trap - ping An -
Bm add9
E/G♯
gels Lord I know this They're trap - ping An -
Bm add9
E/G♯
gels by the Po - to - mac But we're get - ting clos -

G(add9)
Esus2
er now I said we're get-ting clos - er to where they've
Cadd9
G/B
A
Asus4
Cadd9
G/B
gone tell me where they've gone
A
Asus4
Cadd9
G/B
tell me where they've gone
A
Asus4
Cadd9
G/B
A
now it won't be long
rit.

Silent All These Years

Words and Music by Tori Amos

Emaj7
4 fr.
A/E
5 fr.
E
4 fr.
dog won't bite if you sit real still I got the
Emaj7
4 fr.
A/E
5 fr.
E
4 fr.
An - ti - christ in the kitch - en yell - in' at me a - gain
Asus2
B
Yeah I can hear that Been

E
4 fr.
Emaj7
4 fr.
A/E
5 fr.
E
4 fr.
saved a - gain ____ by the gar - bage truck ____ I got
Emaj7
4 fr.
A/E
5 fr.
E
4 fr.
some-thing to say ____ you know but noth - ing ____ comes ______
Emaj7
4 fr.
A/E
5 fr.
E
4 fr.
Yes I know what you think of me you nev - er shut up

Asus2
B
Chorus
Yeah I can hear that But
Aadd9
B
what if I'm ___ a mer - maid in these
melody
Amaj9
B7
jeans of his ___ with her ___ name still on it Hey but

Aadd9
Badd9
I don't care 'cause some - times I said

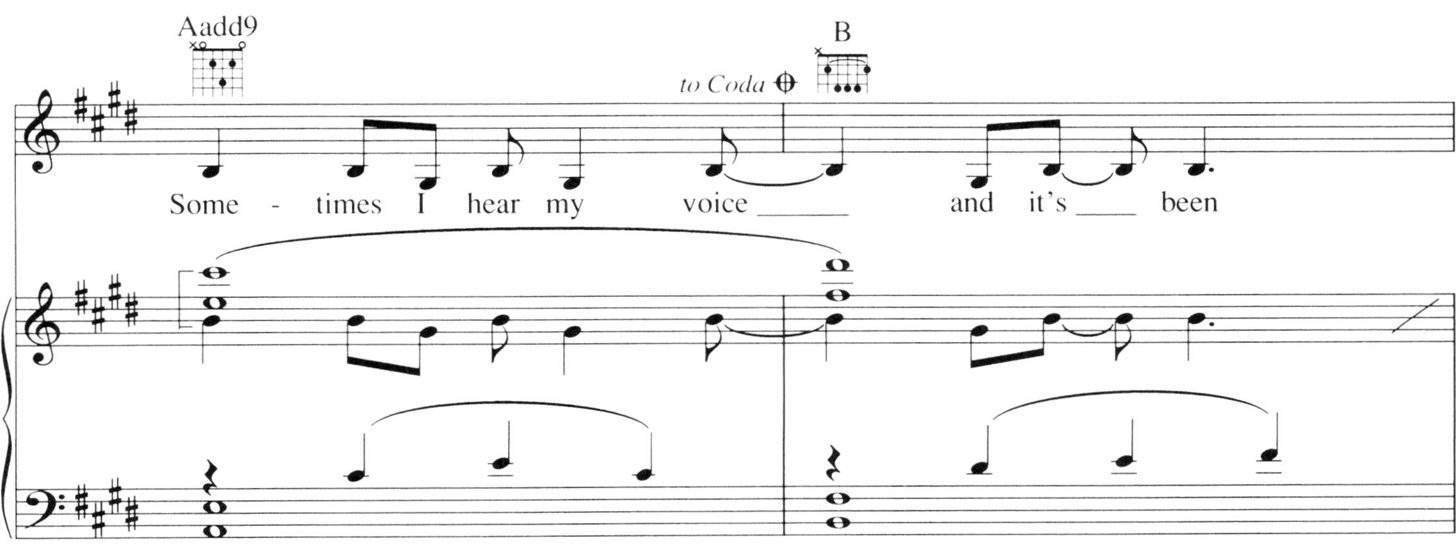
Aadd9
to Coda
B
Some - times I hear my voice and it's been

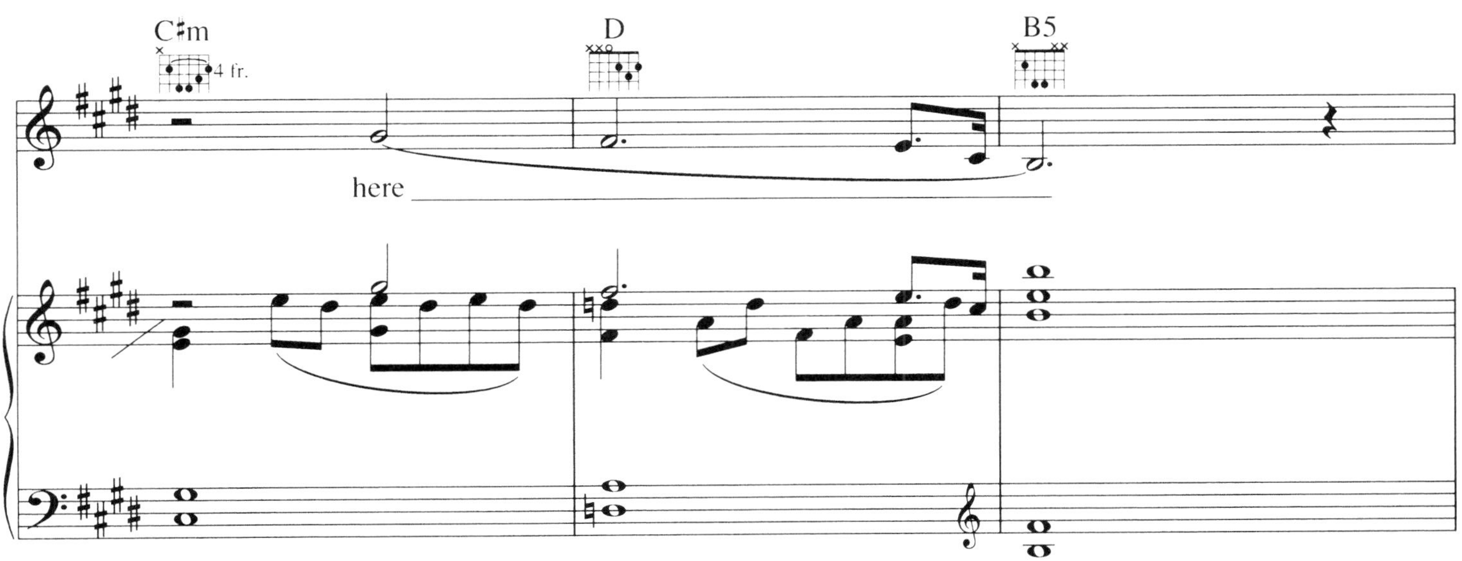
C♯m
4 fr.
D
B5
here

1.
A5
E5
No chord
Si - lent all these years
2. So you
2.
A5
Si - lent all these

E
B/E
A/E
B/F♯
G♯m7
Years go by will I still be wait - ing for
melody
f subito
Aadd9
Bsus4
B
some - bod - y else to un - der - stand
E
B/E
Aadd9/C♯
B
Years go by if I'm stripped of my beau - ty And the

Aadd9
Bsus4
B
or - ange clouds ___ rain - ing in my head ____
E
B
C♯m
4 fr.
B
Years go by will I choke on my tears ____ till
Asus2
E/B
B
fi - nal - ly ____ there is noth - ing left ____

E
4 fr.
B/D♯
4 fr.
A/C♯
B5
One more ca - sual - ty You know we're too
Asus2
Bsus4
D.S. al Coda
eas - y eas - y eas - y 3. Well I
Coda
B
Aadd9
I hear my voice I hear my

B
C♯m
4 fr.
voice and it's been here
D
B5
A5
Si - lent all these
E
G♯m/D♯
4 fr.
years
I've been

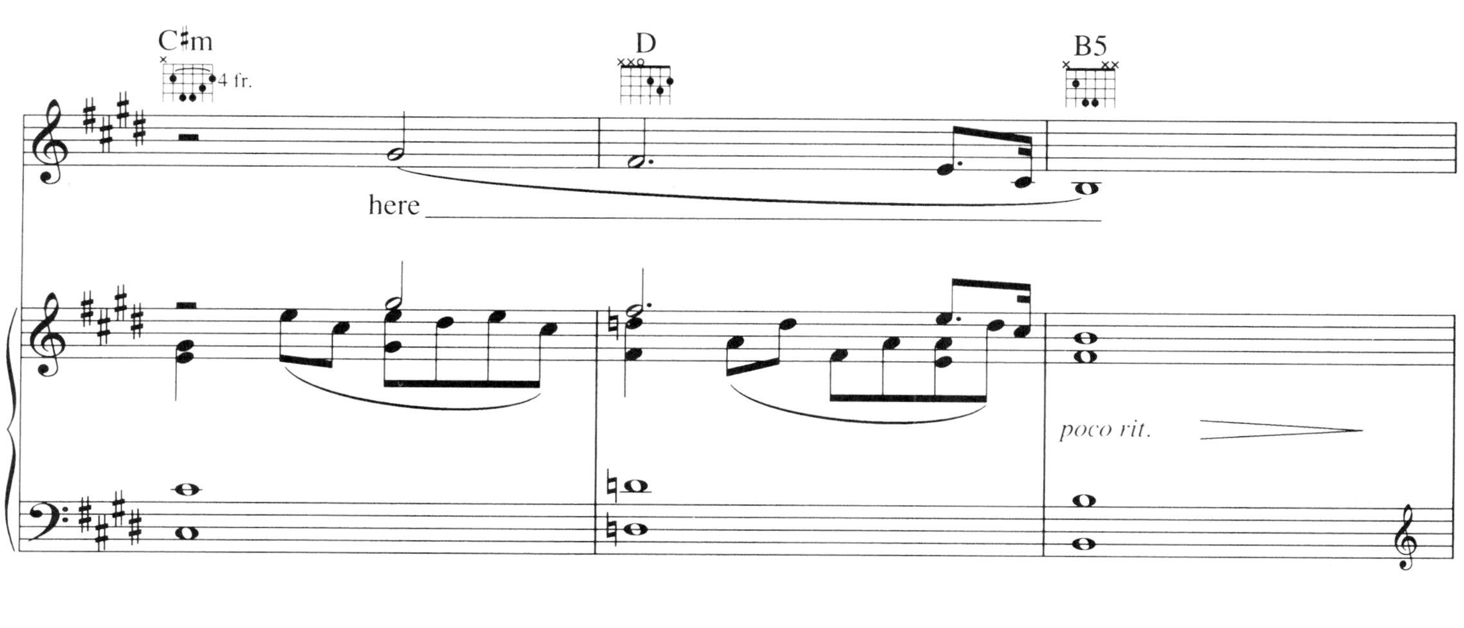

A5
E5

Si - lent all these years

a tempo

E
G

poco cresc.

mf

2. So you found a girl who thinks really deep thoughts
What's so amazing about really deep thoughts
Boy you best pray that I bleed real soon
How's that thought for you

My scream got lost in a paper cup
You think there's a heaven where some screams have gone
I got twenty-five bucks and a cracker
Do you think it's enough...to get us there
Cause

(Chorus to 2nd ending)

(𝄋) 3. Well, I love the way we communicate
Your eyes focus on my funny lip shape
Let's hear what you think of me now
But baby don't look up the sky is falling

Your mother shows up in a nasty dress
It's your turn now to stand where I stand
And everybody lookin' at you
Here take hold of my hand...yeah, I can hear them
But

(Chorus to Coda)

Cornflake Girl

Words and Music by Tori Amos

Am7
C6
D7sus4
Fmaj9
yo heave ho
things are get - ting kind of gross and I go a
pe - di - a
they must - a paid her a nice price she's put - tin' on her
Am7
C6
D
sleep - y time
string bear love
this is not real - ly this - a - this - a - this is not real - ly
hap - pen - ing
Am7
C6
D7sus4
you bet your life it is
Fmaj9
you bet your life it is
C
Dm
C/E
G
Hon - ey you bet your li - fe it's a

D
G
D
G
Peel out the watch - word just peel out the watch - word
L.H.
p
L.H.
Am7
C6
D7sus4
1.
Fmaj9
2. She knows what's
mf
2.
Fmaj9
Am7
C6
D7sus4
Fmaj9
Ne - ver was a corn - flake girl thought that was a good sol - u - tion
Piano Solo
Am7
Dsus4
C
Dsus4
play 4 times

Am7
Dsus4
to Coda
(4th time)
C
Dsus4
play 4 times
Rab - bit
where'd you put the keys girl
Am7
Fmaj9
Gsus4
D7sus4
(vocal 2nd time only)
ah
ah
ah
ah
Am7
Fmaj9
Gsus4
and the man with the gold - en gun thinks he knows so much thinks he
D7sus4
D.S. al Coda
play 4 times
knows so much yeah
Coda
C
N.C.
where'd you put the keys girl

Mary

Words and Music by Tori Amos

Slow, steady 4
Eb5
Eb5
Ab
4fr.
Ab5
4fr.
f
Eb5
Ab
4fr.
F5
Ev - 'ry - bod - y wants some - thing from you
ev - 'ry - bod - y want a piece of Mar - y
mf
Ebsus4
Eb
Ab
4fr.
F5
lush val - ley all dressed in green
just ripe for the pick - ing

Ebsus4
Eb
Ab
4fr.
F5
1. god I want to get you out of here
you can ride in a pink Mus - tang
2. ev - 'ry - bod - y wants you sweet heart
ev - 'ry - bod - y got a dream of glor - y
when I think of what we've done to you
oh Mar - y
can you hear me
Las Ve - gas got a pin - up girl
they got her armed as they buy and sell her
grow - ing up is - n't al - ways fun
they tore your dress and stole your rib - bons
riv - ers of milk run - ning dry
can't you hear the dol - phins cry - ing
N.C.
they see you cry they lick their lips but
but - ter - flies don't be - long in nets
what - 'll we do when our ba - bies scream
fill their mouths with some ac - id rain
oh.

F5
Mar - y can you hear me Mar - y you're bleed - ing
Fadd9
Ebsus4
Eb
Bb
Abass
Mar - y don't be af - raid we're just wak - ing up and I hear
Gm
N.C.
F5
help is on the way Mar - y can you hear me Mar - y, like Jim - i said,
Fadd9
Ebsus4
Eb/G
Eb/B
Mar - y don't be af - raid "'cause e - ven the wind,

B♭
A bass
Gm
E♭
to Coda
e - ven the wind cries your name"
e - ven the wind
mf
1.
A♭5
4fr.
2.
D♭
na na na na na na na na na
na na na na na na na na na na na na na na
cresc. poco a poco
A♭
F5
N.C.
D.S. al Coda
na na na na na na oh, but - ter - flies don't be - long in nets

Coda
B♭
Abass
Gm
E♭
"yes, e - ven the wind cries your name,"
e - ven the wind
B♭
Abass
Gm
E♭
"yes, e - ven the wind cries your name,
e - ven the wind
B♭5
A♭bass
B♭5
A♭bass
cries your name, cries your
B♭5
A♭bass
B♭5
rit.
name, cries your name"
rit.

God

Words and Music by Tori Amos

D7/E
Am
Cbass
Dbass
E♭7/F
B♭m
D♭bass
E♭bass
need a wo - man to look af - ter you
to Coda
God __some- times _ you just don't come through
1. You
C
A
D♭
B♭
make pret - ty dai - sies pret - ty dai - sies ______ love
(2.) tell me you're cra - zy may - be then I'll un - der - stand

D
E♭
C
D♭
I got-ta find find_ find____ what you're do-ing a - bout things_
you got your nine nine_ i-ron___ in the back__seat just_
C/D
D♭/E♭
C
D♭
___ here (a) few witch-es burn - ing gets_ a lit-tle toast-y
___ in case heard you've gone south__ well babe_you love your new four-
A
B♭
D
E♭
here
wheel
I got-ta find find__find_____ why you
D/A
E♭/B♭
Am
B♭m
al - ways go_____ when the wi - (i)nd blows___
p
a tempo

Am
B♭m
Cbass
D♭bass
Dbass
E♭bass
Am
B♭m
mf
D
E♭
Am
B♭m
Will __ you e - ven tell her if you de - cide to __ make the __ sky fall
D
E♭
C
D♭
D
E♭
D.S. al Coda
will __ you e - ven tell her if you de - cide to __ make the __ sky ____
Coda
Am
B♭m
Cbass
D♭bass
Dbass
E♭bass
Am
B♭m
ah ____ ah
p

WINTER

Words and Music by Tori Amos

D5
Eb5
Am7
Bbm7
Bb5
Cb5
G5
Ab5
I get a lit-tle-war-min my heart — when I think of win - ter
I put my hand in my fa - ther's — glove. —
I run off where the driffs get deep - er
Sleep-ing beau - ty
trips me with — a frown —
I hear a voice "You must learn to stand up

D5
Eb5
Am7
Bbm7
Bb5
Cb5
G5
Ab5
for your-self 'cause I can't al - ways be a - round"
He says.
Chorus
F
Gb
Dm
Ebm
Bb
Cb
mp
When you gon - na make up your mind
When you gon - na love you as much
as I do
When you gon - na make up your mind
'Cause things are gon - na
change so fast
All the white hors - es are still in bed
All the white hors - es have gone a - head

Gm F B♭
A♭m G♭ C♭
I tell you that I'll al - ways want you near You say that things
Dm C B♭maj7♯11 C Dm B♭5 G5
E♭m D♭ C♭maj7♯11 D♭ E♭m C♭5 A♭5
to Coda
1.
change my dear
2.
D5 F5 G5 D5 F F5 G5
E♭5 G♭5 A♭5 E♭5 G♭ G♭5 A♭5
dear. 3. Hair is grey and the fires are burn - ing
f
mf
D5 F F5 G5 F5 F
E♭5 G♭ G♭5 A♭5 E♭5 G♭
So man - y dreams on the shelf You say I want - ed

Boys get discovered as winter melts
Flowers competing for the sun
Years go by and I'm here still waiting
Withering where some snowman was.

Mirror mirror where's the crystal palace
But I only can see myself
Skating around the truth who I am
But I know Dad the ice is getting thin.

(Chorus to 2nd ending)

Spark

Words and Music by Tori Amos

E
C
D
she's ad - dict - ed to nic - o - tine patch - es
E
C
D
she's a - fraid of the light in the dark
E
C
D
six - fif - ty - eight are you sure where my spark is
E
C
D
here here here

E
C
D
1. she's con - vinced she could hold back a gla - cier
2. if the Div - ine mas - ter plan is per - fec - tion
E
C
D
but she could - n't keep Ba - by a - live
may - be next I'll give Ju - das a try
E
C
D
doubt - ing if there's a wom - an in there some - where
trust - ing my soul to the ice - cream as - sas - sin

E C D
here here_ here_______________ you
C D G
say you don't want it a - gain and a - gain but you don't don't real - ly
mf
Em C D
mean_ it you say you don't want it this cir - cus we're in but you
G Em C
don't don't real - ly mean_ it you don't don't real - ly

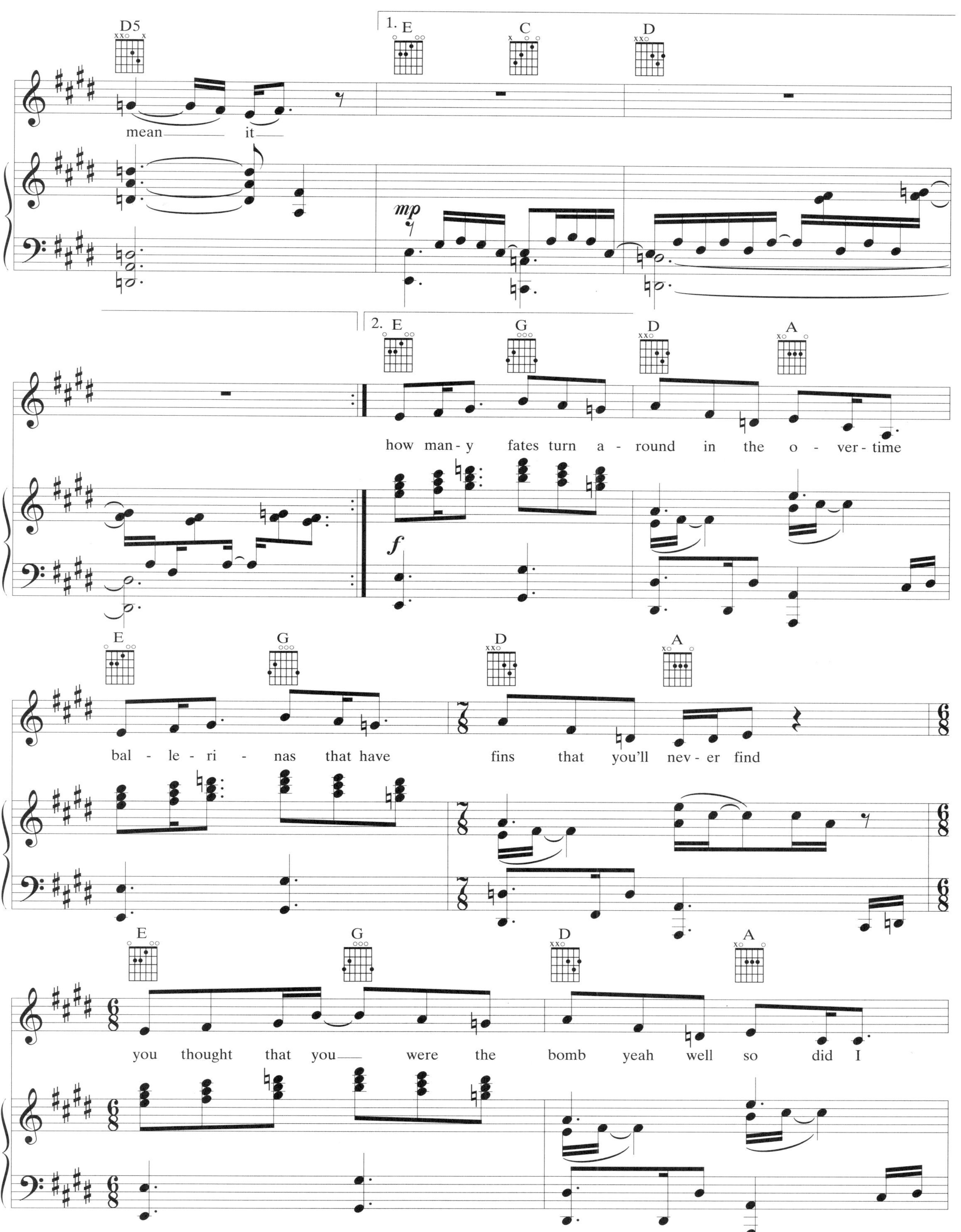
D5
1. E
C
D
mean it
mp
2. E
G
D
A
how man-y fates turn a-round in the o-ver-time
f
E
G
D
A
bal-le-ri-nas that have fins that you'll nev-er find
E
G
D
A
you thought that you were the bomb yeah well so did I

D/C
C
D
E
C
say you don't want it say you don't want it
D
A
E
G
D
A
how man-y fates turn a-round in the o-ver-time
E
G
D
A
bal-le-ri-nas that have fins that you'll nev-er find
E
G
D
A
you thought that you were the bomb yeah well so did I

D/C
C
D
say you don't want it say you don't want it
D/C
D
say you don't want it a - gain and a - gain but you
G
Em
C
don't don't real - ly mean_ it you say you don't want it this
mp
D
G
Em
cir - cus we're in but you don't don't real - ly mean_ it you

C
D5
E
C
don't don't real-ly mean it she's ad-dict-ed to
p
D
E
C
nic-o-tine patch-es she's a-fraid of the
D
A
E
C
light in the dark six-fif-ty-eight are you
D
E
C
D
sure where my spark is here here here
rit.

Way Down

Words and Music by Tori Amos

F
Am
Dm
din - ing here with Son of Sam a hair too much to
D/F#
Fadd9
C
Dm
chat of on the way down gon - na meet a
D/F#
F
Am
great big star gon - na drive his great big car
Dm
D/F#
Fadd9
C
A bit slower
gon - na have it all here on the way down the

C
B°7
Am
Fadd9
C
way
down
the
way
down
R.H.
G/D
Am
Fadd9
C
she
knows
let's
go
the
way
down
R.H.
B°7
Am
the
way
down
the
Fadd9
C
G/D
Am
way
down
she
knows
R.H.

Professional Widow

Words and Music by Tori Amos

G5 G♯5 A5
4 fr
don't blow those
what is termed a
brains yet we got - ta be big boy
land slide of prin - ci - ple pro - por - tion boy
we got - ta be big
it's got - ta be big boy
star fuck - er
just like my Dad - dy
Dsus4

A5
G5
G♯5
A5
G5
G♯5
A5
4 fr
yes star fuck - er
Dsus4
A5
Dsus4
just like my Dad - dy yes sel - ling his ba - by
A5
Dsus4
A5
yes just like my Dad - dy yes gon - na
D5
G5
G♯5
A5
to Coda
strike a deal make him feel like a Con - gress - man

G5
G♯5
A5
4 fr
C
C/G
A5
it runs in the fam - i - ly
it
C
C/G
A5
No chord
(ad-lib.)
G5
G♯5
A5
4 fr
runs in the fam - i - ly
G5
G♯5
A5
4 fr
G5
G♯5
A5
4 fr
G5
G♯5
A5
4 fr
Slow waltz
3
C
F
G
F/G
rest your
shoul - ders
Peach - es and
3
sub. p lightly

C
C7
F
Cream ev - 'ry - where a Ju - das as
G
F/G
C
C7
far as you can see beau - ti - ful
F
G
F/G
C
an - gel call - ing "we
C7
F
G
F/G
C
D.S. al Coda
got ev - 'ry re - run of Mu - ham - mad Al - i"

Coda
G5
G♯5
4 fr
A5
C
C/G
A5
it's run-ning in the fam-i-ly
it
runs in the fam-i-ly
hey ba-by
it's run-ning in the fam-i-ly
it runs in the fam-i-ly
N.C.
(ad-lib.)
Slow waltz
3
A
C
Moth - er Mar - y
chi - na
mf

D
A
white
brown may be
C
swee - ee - eet - er may -
D
A
be swee - ter Moth - er Ma -
C
D
ry chi - na white

A
C
brown may be sweet - er she
D
A
will sup - ply she will sup -
C
G
D
ply she will sup - ply she
A
C
G
D
repeat and fade
will sup - ply sup - ply sup - ply she

Mr Zebra

Words and Music by Tori Amos

Cabaret sleaze

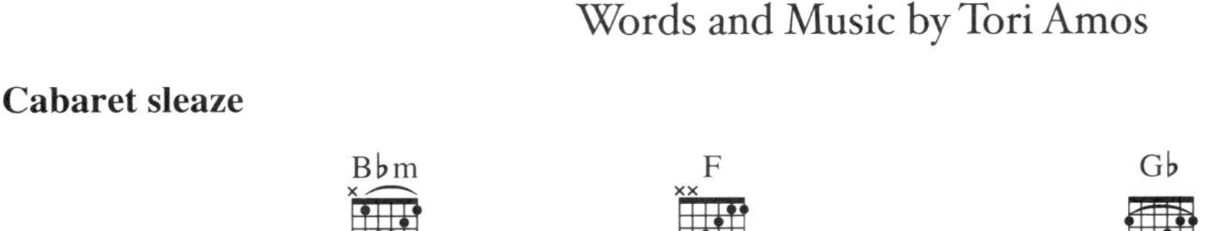

mp

hel - lo Mis - ter Ze - bra can I have your sweat - er 'cause it's

Cm7 F

cold cold cold in my hole hole hole

B♭m F7 G♭ D♭ 4 fr

Rat - a - tou - ille Strych - nine some - times she's a friend of mine with

mf

B♭m
F
Gm7
F/A
a gi - gan - tic whirl - pool that will blow your mind
mp
B♭m
F
B♭m
A♭
D♭
4 fr
hel - lo Mis - ter Ze - bra ran in - to some con - fu - sion with a
Cm7
F
Mis - sus Croc - o - dile - dile - dile
B♭m
F7
G♭
D♭
fur - ry mus - cles march - ing on she thinks she's Kai - ser Wil - helm or
mf

B♭m
F
Gm7
F/A
No chord
a civ - i - lized syl - la - bub __ to blow your mind ______
R.H.
L.H.

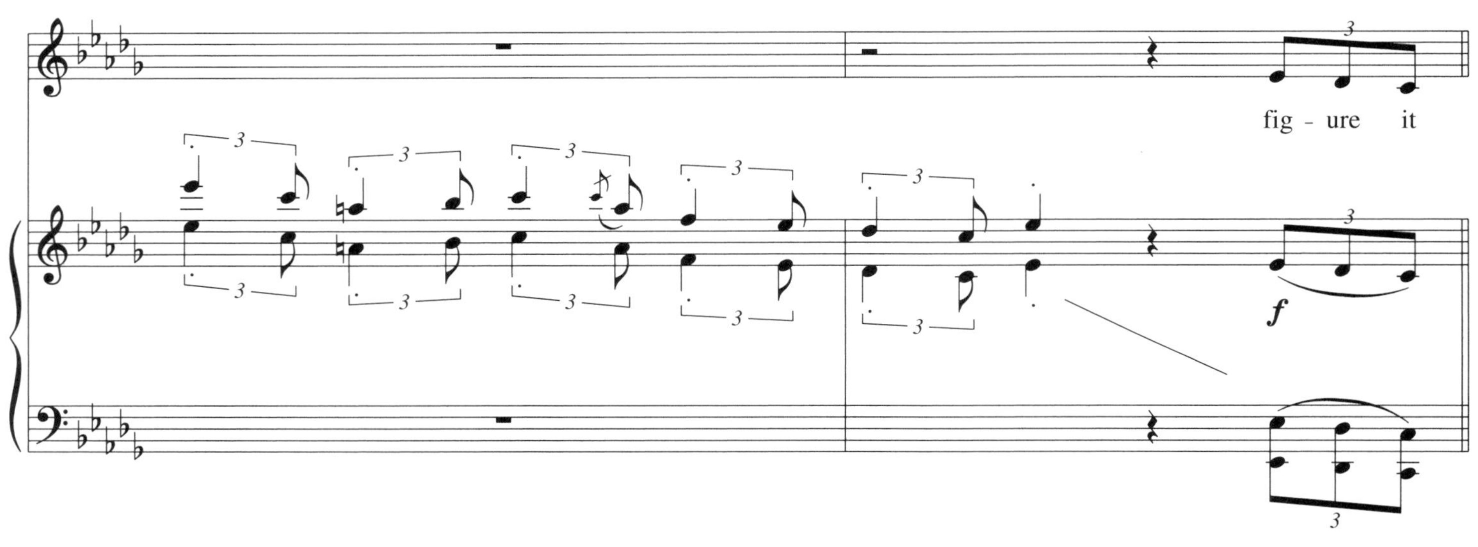
fig - ure it

B♭m
F7
G♭
out she's __ a good - time fel - la ____ she

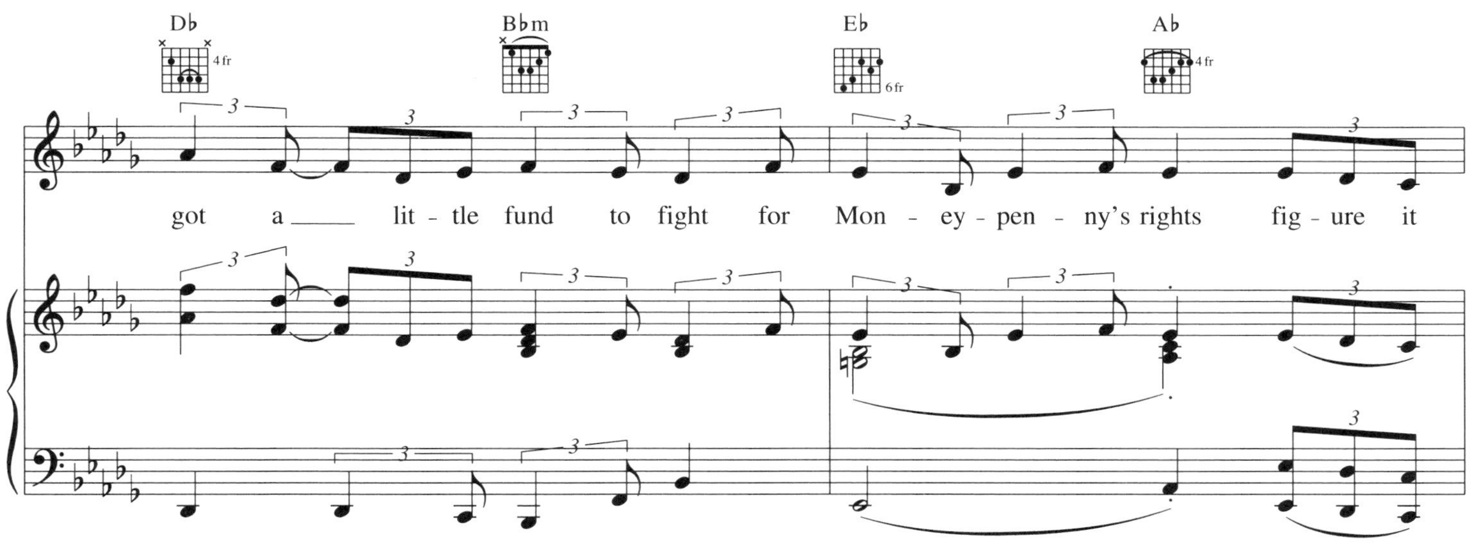
D♭
4 fr
B♭m
E♭
6 fr
A♭
4 fr
got a little fund to fight for Mon-ey-pen-ny's rights fig-ure it

B♭m
F7
G♭
out she's a good-time fel-la too

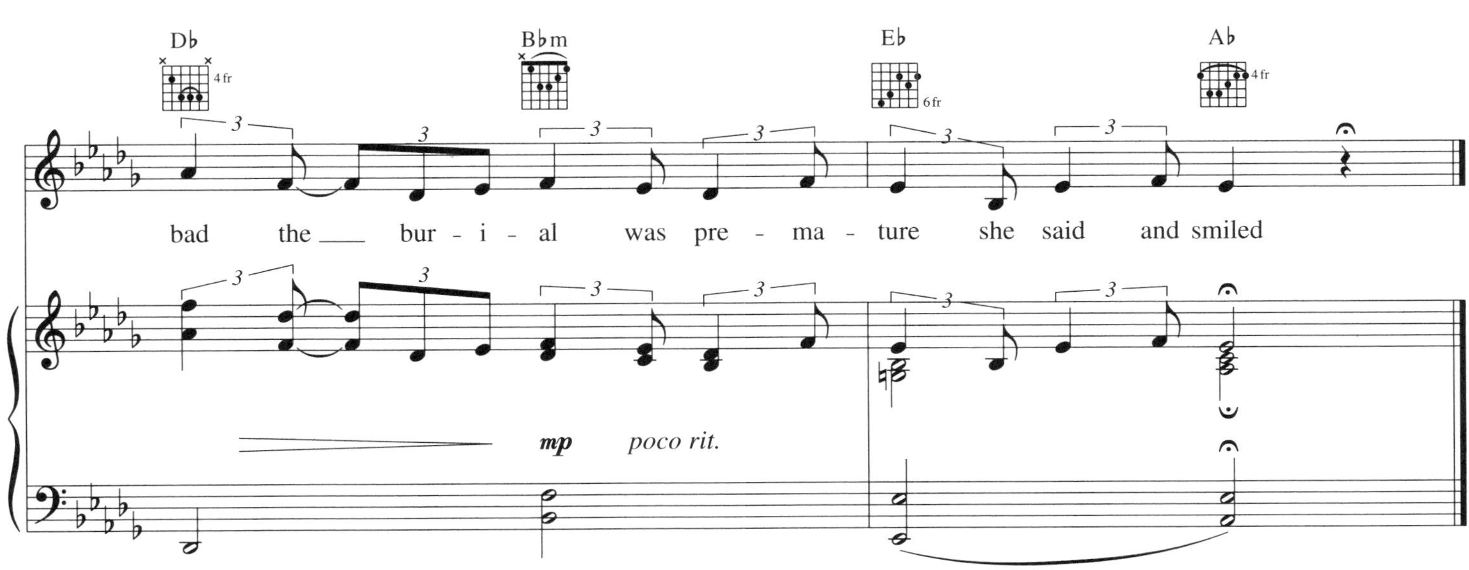
D♭
4 fr
B♭m
E♭
6 fr
A♭
4 fr
bad the bur-i-al was pre-ma-ture she said and smiled
mp
poco rit.

CRUCIFY

Words and Music by Tori Amos

G♯5
4 fr.
A♯5
6 fr.
F♯5
G♯5
4 fr.
bowl-ing ball in my stom-ach I got a de-sert in my mouth
A♯5
6 fr.
F♯5
Fig-ures that my cour - age would choose to sell out now I've been
B
F♯
G♯m
4 fr.
E
look-ing for a sav-ior in these dirt - y streets
F♯
G♯m
4 fr.
E
F♯
Look - ing for a sav - ior be - neath these dirt - y sheets I've been

B
F♯
G♯m
G♯m7/F♯
4 fr.
raising up my hands drive another nail in
Just what
E♯m7♭5
E
Chorus
God needs one more victim
Why do
G♯m
C♯m7
F♯
C♯m7
4 fr.
mf
we crucify ourselves
Every day
I crucify myself
Nothing I do is good e-

G♯m
C♯m7
F♯
C♯m7
4 fr.
nough for you. __ I cru - ci- fy __ my - self Ev - ery ______
G♯m
C♯m7
F♯
day I cru - ci - fy ___ my - self My ___
C♯m
E
heart is sick of be - ing ___ I said my heart is sick of be - ing in
G♯m
B
E
C♯m
chains ______ oh __ oh

G♯m
B
1.
E
C♯m
4 fr.
chains
oh oh
2. to next strain
Fine
Why do
we cru - ci-fy our - selves
repeat and fade
G♯
A♯m
F♯
Please
be
Save
me

B
F♯
G♯
4 fr.
A♯m
B
F♯
I
cry
G♯
4 fr.
A♯m
B
F♯
Ah
ah
B
F♯
G♯m
4 fr.
E
Look-ing for a sav-ior in these dirt-y streets
mp
F♯
G♯m
4 fr.
E
F♯
Look-ing for a sav-ior be-neath these dirt-y sheets I've been

Additional Lyrics

2. Got a kick for a dog beggin' for love
I gotta have my suffering so that I can have my cross
I know a cat named Easter he says "Will you ever learn"
You're just an empty cage girl if you kill the bird

I've been looking for a savior in these dirty streets
Looking for a savior beneath these dirty sheets
I've been raising up my hands, drive another nail in
Got enough guilt to start my own religion

(Chorus to 2nd ending)

ME AND A GUN

Words and Music by Tori Amos

Freely

a capella

Five a. m. Fri-day morn - ing Thurs-day night far from

sleep I'm still up and driv-in' can't go home ob-vi-ous -

ly So I'll just change di - rec- tion 'cause they'll soon know where I

live And I wan-na live got a full tank and some

chips It was me and a gun and a man on my

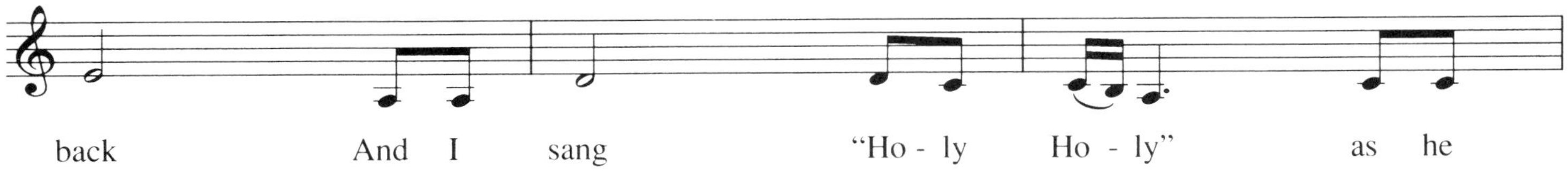
back And I sang "Ho - ly Ho - ly" as he

but-toned down his pants You can laugh it's kind of
fun - ny the things you think in times like these Like I
have- n't seen Bar - ba - dos so I must get out _____ of
this Yes I wore a slink - y red thing Does that
mean I should spread for you your friends your
fa - ther Mis - ter Ed It was me and a gun and a
man on my back But I have - n't seen Bar-

ba - dos so I must get out ___ of this And I
know what this means Me and Je - sus a few years
back used to hang and he said "It's your choice babe Just re-
mem- ber I don't think you'll be back in three days
time so you choose well" Tell me what's right Is it my
right to be on my stom- ach of Fred's Se - ville
Me and a gun and a man on my back But I
have-n't seen Bar - ba - dos so I must get out ___ of this And

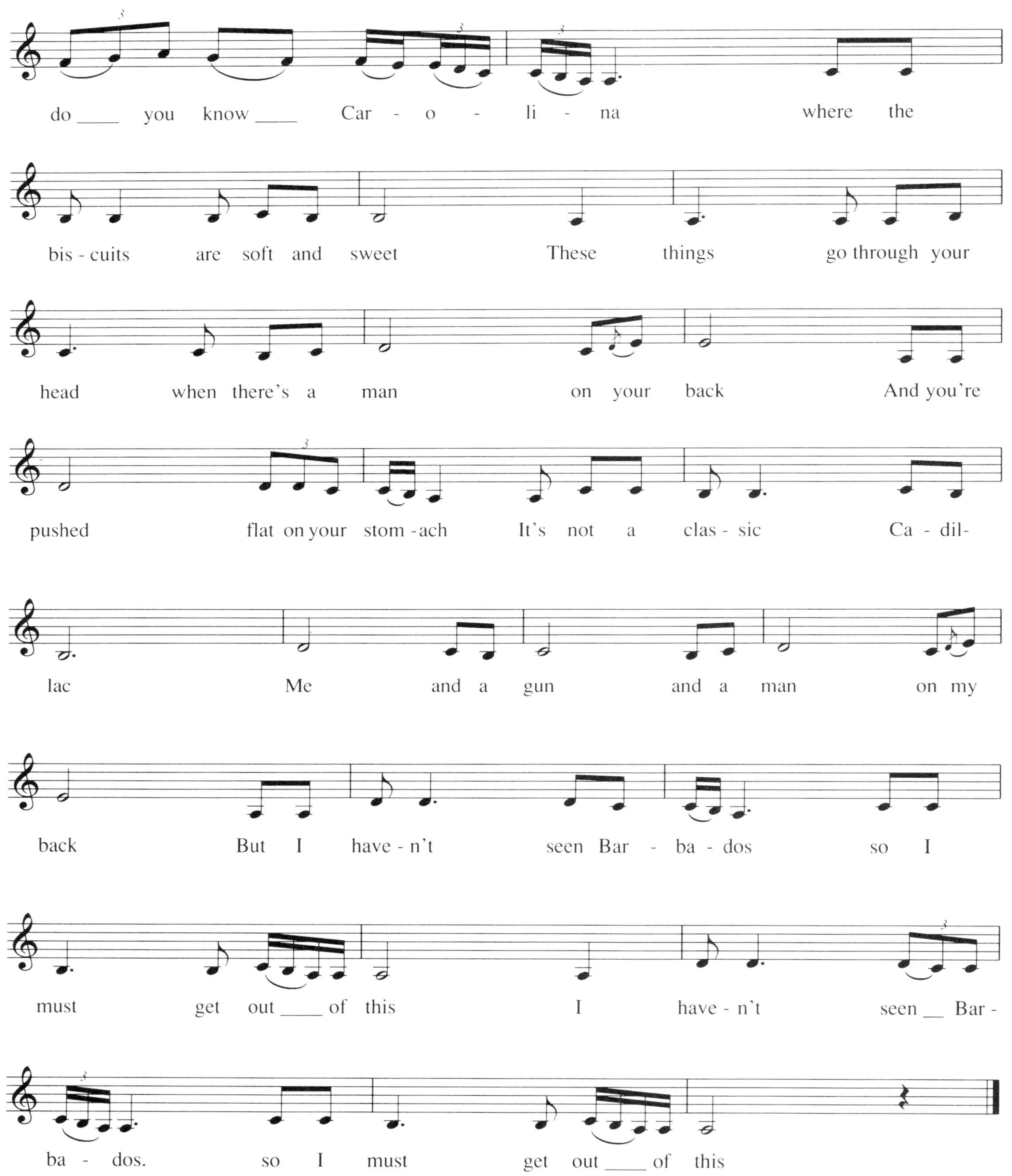
do ___ you know ___ Car - o - li - na where the
bis - cuits are soft and sweet These things go through your
head when there's a man on your back And you're
pushed flat on your stom - ach It's not a clas - sic Ca - dil-
lac Me and a gun and a man on my
back But I have - n't seen Bar - ba - dos so I
must get out ___ of this I have - n't seen __ Bar -
ba - dos. so I must get out ___ of this

Bliss

Words and Music by Tori Amos

E5
B5
G
E5
B5
wonder - der if
I will wan - der
G
E5
B5
G
E5
B5
out
test my teth - er
to
see if I'm still
G
E5
D
A
free from
you
stead - y as
p
f

Bm
G
D
A
Bm
G
it comes right down to you
D
D/C♯
B5
E/G♯
I've said it all so may-be we're a bliss of a-
Em/G
noth-er kind I said a bliss of a-noth-er kind I said

B5
G
E5
B5
G
E5
late -
mp
B5
G
E5
B5
G
E5
ly I'm in to cir-cuit - ry
B5
G
E5
B5
3
what it means to be made of you but not e -

G
E5
B5
G
E5
B5
nough for you and I won - der if
you can bi - lo - cate
G
E5
B5
G
E5
B5
is that what I taste
your su - per - no - va juice
G
E5
you know it's true
I'm part of

D
A
Bm
G
you
steady-y as it comes
right down to you
D/C♯
I've said it all
B5
E/G♯
Em/G
so may-be we're a bliss of a-noth-er kind I said a
f

D
A
Bm
G
D
A
stead - y as it comes right down
Bm
G
D
D/C♯
B5
to you I've said it all so may - be you're a
E/G♯
Em/G
four horse en - gine with a pow - er drive I said a hot ka - chi - na who wants

E5
into mine I said take it take it with your ter-ra-ter-ra-cide I said a
D A Bm G D A
stead-y as it comes right down
f
Bm G D D/C♯ B5
to you I've said it all so may-be we're a

E/G♯
Em/G
bliss_ of a - noth - er kind_ I said a bliss_ of a -
E5
noth - er kind_ I said a bliss_ of a - noth - er kind_ I said a
E5/F♯
E5/D
E/G♯
Em/G
rit.
bliss_ of a bliss_ of a bliss_ of a - noth - er kind.

Playboy Mommy

Words and Music by Tori Amos

Am
F
C
then the ba - by came be - fore I found the mag - ic how to
G
Am
F
keep her hap - py I nev - er was the fan - ta - sy of
C
G
Am
what you want want - ed me to be
Don't
mf
F
C
G
judge me so harsh lit - tle girl so you got a play - boy mom - my

Am
F
C
but when you tell 'em my name you wan-na cross that bridge
G
Am
F
all on your own lit-tle girl they'll do you no harm
C
G
Am
1st time to Coda
2nd time to Coda
cause they know your play-boy mom-my but when you
F
C
G
tell 'em my name from here to Bir-ming-ham I got a few friends

Am
F
C
G
mp
I nev-er was there was there when it counts I get my way you're
so like me you seem a-shamed a-shamed that I was
a good friend of A-mer-i-can sol-diers I'll say it loud here

F
C
G
D.S. al Coda
by your grave those an - gels can't ev - er take my place
Coda
Am
F
C
but when you tell 'em my name you tell 'em my name
G
Am
F
C
I got a few friends
G
Am
F
Some - where where the or - chids grow
mp

C
G
Am
I can't find those church bells that played when you
F
Am
Em
F
died played Glo - ri - a talk - in' 'bout
p
C
G
D.S. al Coda
Coda
Am
Ho - san - ah
bit I'll be home
F
C
G/C
3fr.
I'll be home to take you in my arms
rit.

Baker Baker

Words and Music by Tori Amos

F♯6
B
C♯(add9)
E(add9)
gone to L. A. _ he says that be - hind _ my eyes I'm hid - ing
your next pa - rade _ you came to make sure _ that I'm not run - ning
G♯m
4 fr.
E(add9)
F♯6
B
C♯(add9)
and _ he tells me I pushed him a - way _ that my heart's been hard to find _
well I ran from him _ in all kinds of ways _ guess it was his turn this time _
E(add9)
Bmaj7/F♯
E(add9)
here there must be some - thing
time thought I'd made friends _ with
mf
Bmaj7/F♯
E(add9)
Bmaj7/F♯
E(add9)
here there must be some - thing here
time thought we'd be fly - ing

1.
2.
F♯
E
here
may - be not this
E
G♯m
E(add9)
F♯
B
4 fr.
time
Bak - er Bak - er
bak-ing a cake
p
mp a tempo
C♯(add9)
E(add9)
G♯m
E(add9)
make me a day
make me whole a-gain
and I won - der
F♯6
B
C♯(add9)
E(add9)
rit.
if he's o - kay
if you see him say hi

TEAR IN YOUR HAND

Words and Music by Tori Amos

Bsus4
B5
E5
Esus2
say you don't _ wan-na stay to - geth- er ___ an - y - more
Bsus4
B5
E5
Esus2
Let me take a deep breath babe if you
Bsus4
B5
E5
Esus2
No chord
need me me and Neil 'll be _____ hang - in' out with the dream king
Bsus4
B5
E5
Esus2
Neil says hi by the way I don't be -

Bsus4
B5
E5
Esus2
lieve ___ you're leav - in' 'cause me and Charles Man - son like the same ice
cream I think it's that girl ___ And I think
melody
G♯m
4 fr.
E
there're piec - es of me ___ you've nev - er seen ___ May - be she's just
piec - es of me ___ you've nev - er seen well

Bsus4
B5
E5
Esus2
All the world is all
all I am The
black of the black - est o - cean And that
tear in your hand

Bsus4
B5
E5
Esus2
All the world is dang -
a - lin' dang - a - lin' dang - a - lin' for me Dar - lin' you
B
G♯m
4 fr.
E
No chord
don't know the pow - er that you have with that
tear in your hand.

Bsus4
B5
to Coda
E5
Esus2
tear ___ in your ___ hand
F♯
F♯sus4
F♯
A
Asus4
A
May - be ___ I __ ain't _ used to
may - bes ___ smash - ing in a cold room _
___ cut - ting my _ hands up ev - ery time I touch you

F♯ F♯sus4 F♯ A
May be maybe it's
G♯m E
time to wave goodbye now
G♯m E F♯
Time to wave goodbye now
Bsus4 B5 E
Caught a ride with the moon I
4 fr.
mp

Bsus4
B5
E
know __ I know you well well bet - ter than I used to
Bsus4
B5
Haze all cloud - ed up my mind in a
E
daze of the why it could - 've nev - er been so you
Bsus4
B5
say and I say you know __ you're full of wish and your

E
D.S. al Coda
"ba - by ba - by ba - by ba - bies" I tell you
melody
Coda
E5
Esus2
E5
G♯m
4 fr.
hand With that tear in your
E5
Esus2
Bsus4
B5
hand
E5
Bsus4
B5
hand
hand

Sweet Dreams

Words and Music by Tori Amos

Bb5
Ab5
4 fr
Bb5
mf
1. "Lie, lie, lies ev - 'ry-where," said the fa - ther to the son your
2.,3. (D.S.) See additional lyrics
pep-per-mint breath gon-na choke 'em to death dad-dy watch your lit-tle black sheep run he got a

Ab5
Bb5
kni, - kni, - knives in his back ev-'ry time he o - pens up you say, "he
Ab5
Bb5
got-ta be strong if he wan-na be a man" mis-ter I don't know how you can have
Bb
Ab
Bb
sweet dreams
Ab
Bb
sweet dreams

Db5
Ab
Bb5
4 fr
you say you say you say that you have 'em
I say that you're a li - ar
Bb
sweet
dreams
sweet
dreams

Ab
Bb
Db5
Ab
Bb
Db
Eb
go on, go on, go on, go on and dream your house is on
Bb5
Ab5
Bb5
N.C.
fire
come a - long
Bb5
to Coda
Ab5
Bb5
D.S. al Coda
now

Additional lyrics

2. land, land of liberty
we're run by a constipated man
when you live in the past
you refuse to see when your
daughter come home nine months pregnant
with five billion points of light
gonna shine 'em on the face of your friends
they got the earth in a sling
they got the world on her knees
they even got your zipper in between their teeth

3. well, well, summer wind been catching up with me
"elephant mind, missy you don't have
you forgettin' to fly,
darlin', when you sleep"
I got a hazy lazy Susan
takin' turns all over my dreams
I got lizards and snakes runnin' through my body.
Funny how they all have my face.

Jackie's Strength

Words and Music by Tori Amos

Bm
A/G
hey Jack - ie yeah strength
A
D
A
G
Bou - vier till her wed - ding day shots rang out the
Bm
A
G
po - lice came ma - ma layed me on the front lawn and
D
A
D
prayed for Jack - ie's strength feel - ing old by
mf

A
G
Bm
twen - ty - one
nev - er
thought my
day
would come
my
A
G
brides - maids
get - ting
laid
I
D
Asus4
A
Asus4
prayed
for
Jack - ie's
strength
make me laugh
Em
D
F♯m
say you know
what you want
you

F♯
B/D♯
6fr.
B
said we were the real thing so I show
Em
D
F♯m
you some more and I learn what
F♯
B/D♯
6fr.
B
black mag - ic can do make me laugh
Em
D
F♯m
say you know you can turn

F♯
B/D♯
6fr.
B
Em
me in - to the real thing so I show you some more
D
F♯m
to Coda
and I learn
D
A
G
stick - ers licked on lunch box - es wor - ship - ping Dav - id
Bm
A
G
Cas - sid - y yeah I mooned him once on Don - na's box she's

D
A
D
still in re - cov - er - y
sleep - o - vers Beene's
A
G
got some pot you're on - ly pop - u - lar with an -
Bm
A
G
o - rex - ia so I turn my - self in - side out in
D
A
Asus4
A
D.S. al Coda
hope some - one will see will see make me laugh

Coda
D
Asus4
hey Jack - ie yeah hey Jack - ie yeah
Bm
G
D
hey Jack - ie yeah strength hey Jack - ie yeah
Asus4
Bm
A/G
hey Jack - ie yeah strength
D
A
G
I got lost on my wed - ding day typ - i - cal the
p

A
po - lice came oh but vir - gins al - ways
G
D
A
get back - stage no mat - ter what they've got to say if you
D
A
G
love e - nough you'll lie a lot guess they did in
mf
Bm
A
G
cam - e - lot ma - ma's wait - ing on my front lawn I

D
Asus4
A/G
pray I pray I pray for Jack - ie's strength
A
Em
strength make me laugh say you know
D
F♯m
F♯
what you want you said we were the real
B/D♯
6fr.
B
Em
thing so I show you some more

D
F♯m
and I learn
D
hey Jack - ie yeah hey Jack - ie yeah
Bm
G
D
hey Jack - ie yeah strength hey Jack - ie yeah
Bm
G
hey Jack - ie yeah hey
rit.
pp

Snow Cherries From France

Words and Music by Tori Amos

E A/E E Cmaj7
F B♭/F F D♭maj7
call Can you launch rock-ets from here Boy I've done it for
call They look like pi-rates from here Boy I've been one for
mf
D Cmaj7
E♭ D♭maj7
years right o-ver my
years just keep-ing my head
And when I prom-ised my
D
E♭
hand he prom-ised me back snow cher-ries from France
Cadd9 D Gadd9 Em Cadd9 D
D♭add9 E♭ A♭add9 Fm D♭add9 E♭
All that sum-mer we trav-eled the world Nev-er leav-ing his

Gadd9
Em
Cadd9
D
A♭add9
Fm
D♭add9
E♭
own back garden
Girls I did-n't know just
what he could be
Oh but he let me go
sail-ing
1.
A
D/A
B♭
E♭/B♭
2.
A6
A7
B♭6
B♭7
sail-ing

E
F♯m7
Em/G
Gmaj7
A
F
Gm7
Fm/A♭
A♭maj7
B♭
f
E
A/E
E
F♯m7
Em/G
F
B♭/F
F
Gm7
Fm/A♭
And then one day he said girl it's been nice
p
Gmaj7
A
E
A/E
E
F♯m7
A♭maj7
B♭
F
B♭/F
F
Gm7
Oh but I have to go sail-ing With cin-na-mon lips that did
Em/G
Gmaj7
A
E
Fm/A♭
A♭maj7
B♭
F
not match his eyes Oh then he let me go
rit.

Pretty Good Year

Words and Music by Tori Amos

F
C
F
C
G♭
D♭
G♭
D♭
heard the e - ter - nal foot - man bought him-self a
F
C
F
C
G♭
D♭
G♭
D♭
bike to ___ race and
B♭sus2
Csus4
C
C♭sus2
D♭sus4
D♭
Greg he writes let-ters and burns his C ___ Ds they
Dm7
E♭m7
say you were some-thing in those form - a - tive years
cresc.

B♭sus2
C♭sus2
Csus4
D♭sus4
C
D♭
hold on - to no - thing as fast as you can
mf
F
G♭
C
D♭
Dm
E♭m
B♭
C♭
well still pret - ty good
F
G♭
C
D♭
Dm
E♭m
B♭
C♭
year ah pret - ty good
F
G♭
F
D♭
Dm
E♭m
B♭
C♭
mf

F
C
G♭
D♭
May - be a bright sand - y beach is gon - na bring you
mp
back __ back __ back ____
may - be not __ so now you're off you're gon - na see A -
me - ri - ca well let me tell you some-thing a-bout A - ne- na- ne -
cresc.

B♭
C♭
Fbass
G♭bass
na - ne - na - ne - na - ne - na A - me - ri - ca
f marcato
F
G♭
C
D♭
Dm
E♭m
mp
B♭
C♭
F
G♭
C
D♭
Dm
E♭m
pret - ty __ good year ah
B♭
C♭
F
G♭
C
D♭
Dm
E♭m
B♭
C♭
pret- ty __ good

B♭sus2
C♭sus2
C
D♭
some things are
p
Dm7
E♭m7
B♭sus2
C♭sus2
melt - ing now
C
D♭
some things are
Dm7
E♭m7
B♭sus2
C♭sus2
melt - ing now well
cresc.

E♭5
E5
G♭bass
Gbass
A♭bass
4 fr.
Abass
hey
what's it gon- na
take
till my
ba - by's al - right what's it gon- na
take
till my
ba - by's al - right
F
G♭
C
D♭
Dm
E♭m
B♭
C♭
ah

F C Dm B♭
G♭ D♭ E♭m C♭
and
Csus4 B♭sus2
D♭sus4 C♭sus2
Greg he writes let-ters with his birth-day pen some-
F/A Dm7
G♭/B♭ E♭m7
times he's a-ware that they're_ draw-ing him in
B♭sus2 Csus4
C♭sus2 D♭sus4
Lu-cy was pret-ty your best friend a-greed___

F
C
Dm
B♭
G♭
D♭
E♭m
C♭
well
still
pret - ty __ good
F
C
Dm
B♭
G♭
D♭
E♭m
C♭
year
ah _______
pret - ty __ good
F
C
Dm
B♭
C
G♭
D♭
E♭m
C♭
poco rit.
D♭
ah _______
pret- ty __ good year
pp

Honey

Words and Music by Tori Amos

E5
Em/G
C
Bm/D
some-times I can hold my tongue, some-times not, when you just
G
Em
C
Bm/D
skip-to-loo my dar-lin' and you know what you're do-in' so
Gmaj7
Em
C
G
don't e-ven you're just too used to my hon-ey now
mp
Bm add9
C
G
you're just too used to my hon-ey
R.H.

Bm add9
E5
p
with pedal
Em/G
1. and I think I could leave your world
2. (D.S.) turn back one last time
C
Bm/D
E5
if she was the bet - ter girl
love to watch those cow - boys ride
p
with pedal
C
Bm/D
so when we died I tried to bribe the
but cow-boys know cow - girls ride

G
Em
C
un - der - tak - er
'cause I'm not sure
on the In - dian side
and you know
D
Gmaj7
Em
what you're do - in' or the rea - sons
what you're do - in' so don't e - ven
C
G
Bm add9
you're just too used to my hon-ey now
mp
R.H.
C
G
Bm add9
you're just too used to my hon-ey
hey, yeah

C
G
Bm add9
to Coda
you're just too used to my hon-ey now
cresc.
G
D
A
don't both-er coming down
mf
C
G
Em
A
I made a friend of the west-ern sky
don't both-er coming down
C
G
E5
you al-ways like your ba-bies tight
p

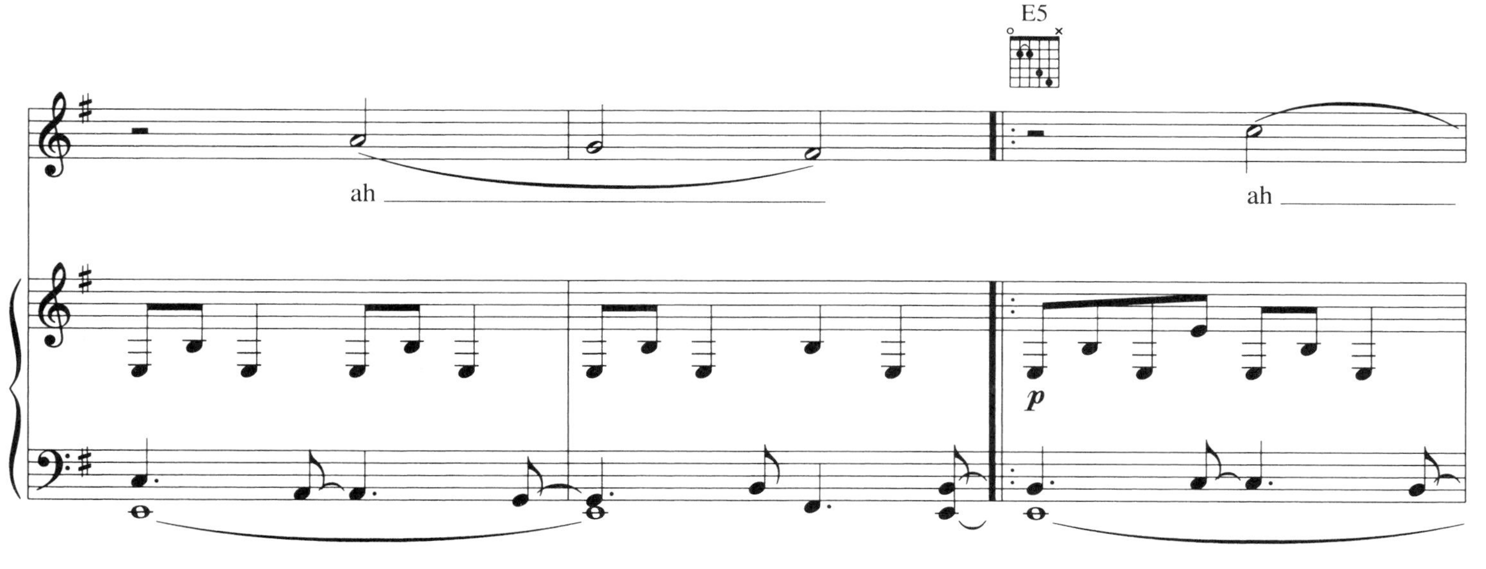
E5
ah
ah
p

D.S. al Coda
ah

Coda
Bm add9
C
G
B bass
you're just too used to my hon-ey
rit.

NORTHERN LAD

Words and Music by Tori Amos

Dadd9
5fr.
E
Esus4
I thought we'd be o - kay
me and my mo - las - ses
F♯m
E
1. But I feel some - thing is wrong
But I
2. I feel the west in you
and I
mf
F♯m
E
feel this cake just is - n't done
feel is fall - ing a - part too
Dadd♯11
5fr.
Dsus2
F♯madd11
Don't say that you Don't and if you could see me now
mp
mf

D
E
F♯madd11
said if you could see me now
D
F♯madd11
girls you've got to know when it's time to turn the
D
to Coda
A
page when you're on - ly wet be - cause of the
E
C♯madd9
4fr.
rain be - cause of

Dadd9
5fr.
A
'cause of the rain
E
C♯madd9
4fr.
Dadd♯11
5fr.
because of
Aadd9
Bmadd9
mp
he don't show much those days
it gets so fuck - ing cold
Dadd9
5fr.
E
Esus4/D
I loved his se - cret plac - es
but I can't go an - y - more

Aadd9
Bm add9
"you change like su - gar cane"
says my north - ern lad
Dadd9
5fr.
E
Esus4
D.S. al Coda
I guess you go too far when pi - an - os try to be guit - tars and
Coda
A
E
wet be - cause of the rain when you're on - ly
F♯madd11
E
wet be - cause of the rain be - cause of

C♯madd9
4fr.
Dadd9
5fr.
A
of
'cause
of
the
E
C♯madd9
4fr.
Dadd9
5fr.
rain
be - cause
of
be - cause
A
E
of
the
rain
be - cause
of
C♯madd9
4fr.
Dadd9
5fr.
A
of
the
rain
rit.

Putting The Damage On

Words and Music by Tori Amos

G
F
G
an - y - one ___ know ___ why
you play with an or - ange ___
Am
F
G bass
C
rind you say you packed my things and di -
G
F
G
vid - ed what was ___ mine
you're off to the moun - tain ___
F
G
Am
top I say her skin - ny legs ___ could use ___ sun but

F6
C
G
now I'm wish - ing for my best im - pres - sion
F
G
F
of my best An - gie Dick - in - son but now
G
Am
F
I've got to wor - ry 'cause boy you
F6
C
G
still look pret - ty when you're put - ting the dam - age

Am
F
C
G
on yes when you're put - ting the dam - age
C
on
cresc.
R.H.
Cadd9
D/C
C
to Coda
mf
don't make me scratch on your door I nev - er left
F
G bass
F
sub. p

G
F
G
you for a Ban - jo
I on - ly just turned a -
Am
F
G bass
C
round for a poo - dle and a cor - vette and my
G
F
G
im - pres - sion of my best An - gie Dick - in - son
F
G
Am
but now I've got to wor - ry 'cause

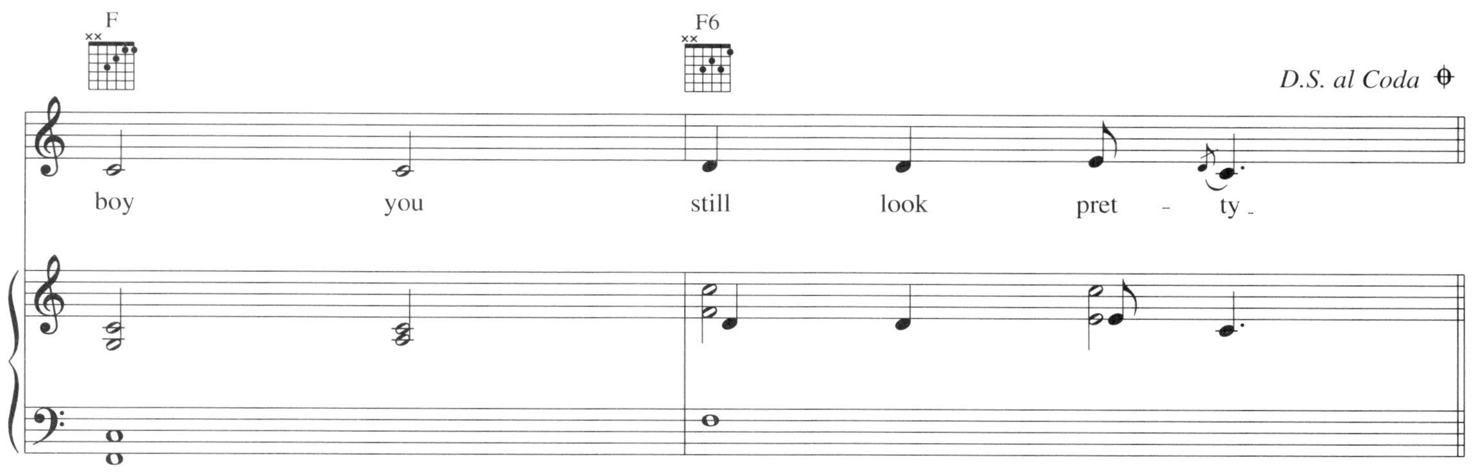
F
F6
D.S. al Coda
boy you still look pret - ty

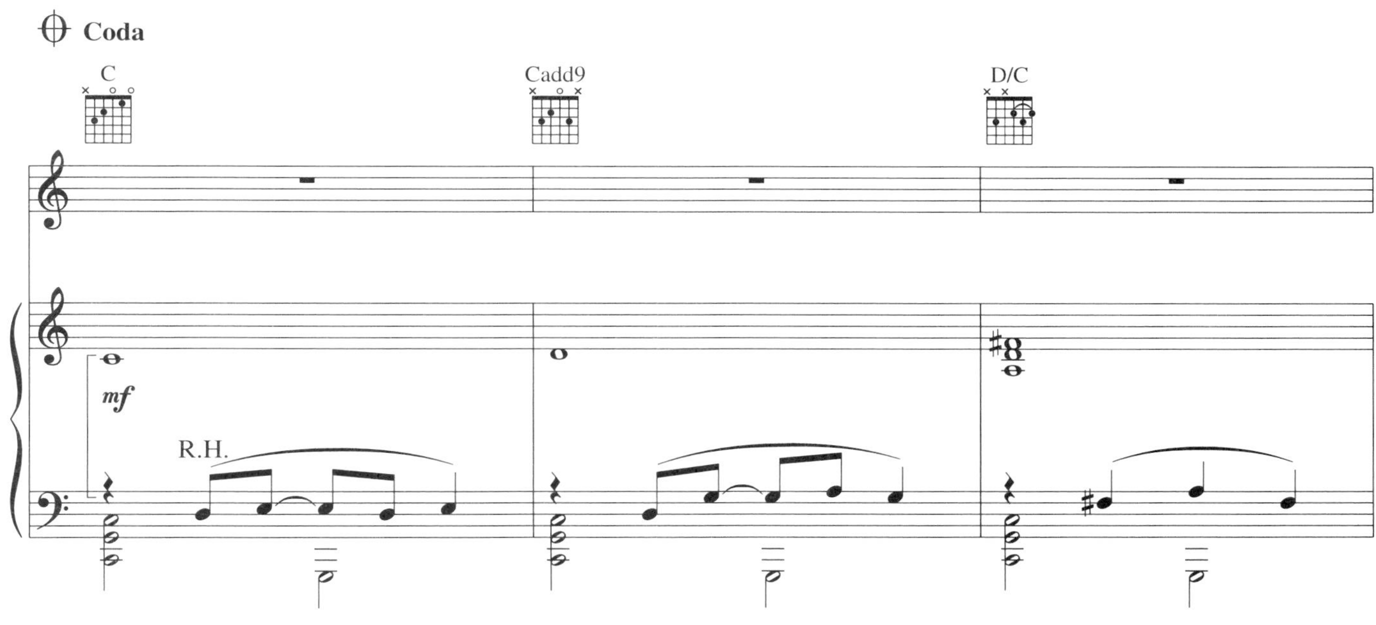
Coda
C
Cadd9
D/C
mf
R.H.

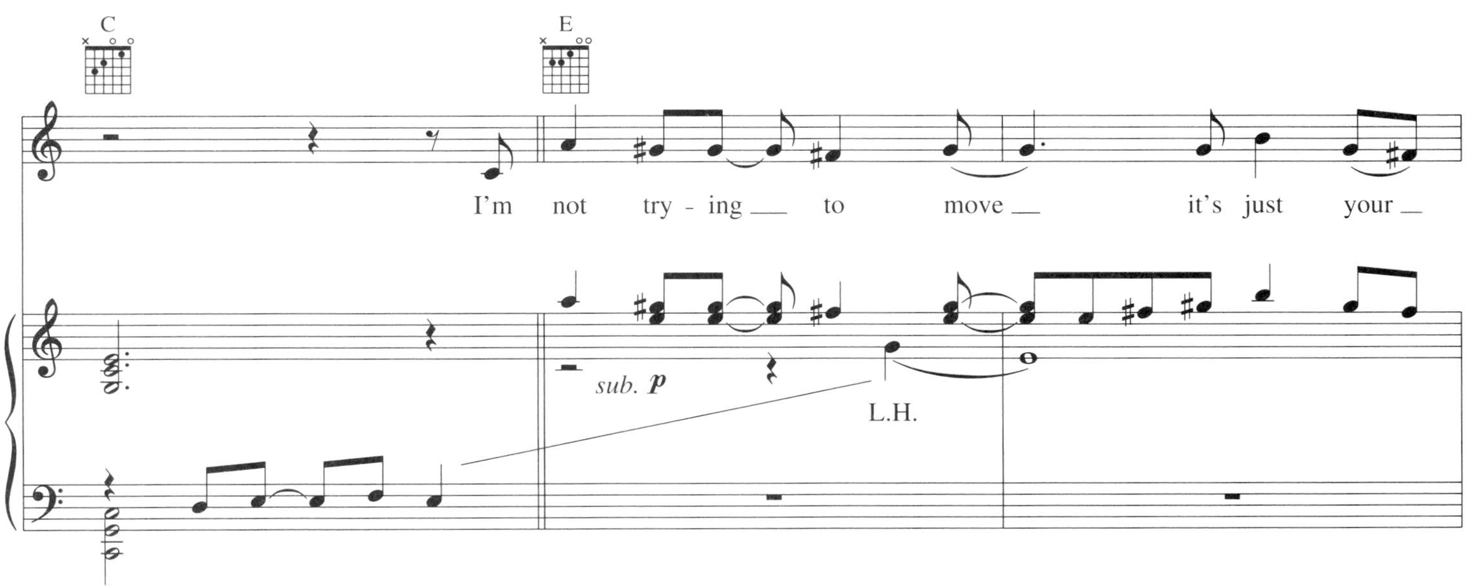
C
E
I'm not try - ing to move it's just your
sub. p
L.H.

Bm
E
ghost passing through I said I'm try - ing not to
move it's just your ghost passing through it's just your
D/A
No chord
ghost passing through and now I'm quite sure
C
G
F
there's a light in your pla - toon I
a tempo

G
F
G
nev - er seen a light move __ like __ yours can __ do to
Am
F6
C
me so now I'm wish - ing_ for my best _
G
F
G
__ im - pres - sion ___ of my best An - gie Dick - in - son __
F
G
Am
__ but now __ I've got to wor - ry __ cause

F
F6
poco rit.
C
a tempo
boy you still look pret - ty _ to me but I've _
poco rit.
a tempo
G
F
G
_ got a place _ to go I've got a tick - et to your late
cresc.
F
G
Am
show _ and now _ I've got to wor - ry _ cause e - ven
f
F
F6
C
still you sure are pret - ty_ when you're put -
p

G
Am
F
G bass
ting the dam - age on yes
C
G
Am
when you're put - ting the dam - age on you're
F
C
G
poco rit.
a tempo
rit.
just so pret - ty when you're put - ting the dam - age
poco rit.
a tempo
rit.
C
on